LOST IN THE SYSTEM

To Beth -
Happy Reading :)

Blessings,
Nancy Jo

Advance Praise

Nancy Jo Wilson has found a way to weave together science fiction, faith, and contemporary society in surprising and page turning ways. I can honestly say I've rarely seen a male protagonist so well-rendered by a female author.

—**Hunter Baker**, Dean of Arts and Sciences Union University

Lost in the System takes us on a delightfully wild ride that shows us ourselves and the unpredictable God who seeks us out. Through the eyes of a 24th century, time-traveling conman, Nancy had me hooked from the very first chapter!

—**Mark DeVries**, founder of Ministry Architects

Lost in the System is an entertaining, insightful, and fast-paced time-travel book with a twist. Author Nancy Wilson weaves a unique and fascinating story around Smullian O›Toole, a likable "grifter" who has landed in trouble with 24th-century legal authorities. Smully's time-traveling adventures are sometimes hilarious and often poignant as he barrels toward a surprising and powerful resolution. Well done!

—**Kay DiBianca**, award-winning author of
The Watch on the Fencepost and *Dead Man's Watch.*

Science fiction is not my go-to genre when choosing a new book: I prefer a good crime mystery. Yet, I was intrigued by the summary of *Lost in the System*. I'm so glad I opted to read it! This story punches in from the first paragraph, introducing the reader to Smullian O'Toole, a young grifter from the twenty-fourth century. He readily admits being guilty and is comfortable participating in a new method of prisoner rehabilitation. The author skillfully creates a character who is likeable, interesting, irreverent, intelligent, and adaptive in his circumstances. The story takes on a deeper edge when a "glitch" in this future-based system creates a multifaceted mystery. There are no dull moments in this fiction. Most amazing for me was that embedded in this well-written, sci-fi mystery are thoughts and truths about faith, strength, hope and love that have kept me thinking long after the last page was turned.

—**Judy Karge**, author of *A Light In the Dark: Reflection on Proverbs*

LOST
IN THE
SYSTEM
A NOVEL

NANCY JO WILSON

NEW YORK

LONDON • NASHVILLE • MELBOURNE • VANCOUVER

LOST IN THE SYSTEM
A NOVEL

© 2021 **NANCY JO WILSON**

Published in New York, New York, by Morgan James Publishing. Morgan James is a trademark of Morgan James, LLC. www.MorganJamesPublishing.com

Publisher's Note: This novel is a work of fiction. Names, characters, places, and incidents are either products of the author's imagination or used fictitiously. All characters are fictional, and any similarity to people living or dead is purely coincidental.

Morgan James BOGO™

A **FREE** ebook edition is available for you or a friend with the purchase of this print book.

CLEARLY SIGN YOUR NAME ABOVE

Instructions to claim your free ebook edition:
1. Visit MorganJamesBOGO.com
2. Sign your name CLEARLY in the space above
3. Complete the form and submit a photo of this entire page
4. You or your friend can download the ebook to your preferred device

ISBN 978-1-63195-456-6 paperback
ISBN 978-1-63195-457-3 eBook
Library of Congress Control Number:
2020924017

Cover Design by:
Chris Treccani
www.3dogdesign.net

Morgan James PUBLISHING **Builds** **with... Habitat for Humanity®** Peninsula and Greater Williamsburg

Morgan James is a proud partner of Habitat for Humanity Peninsula and Greater Williamsburg. Partners in building since 2006.

Get involved today! Visit
MorganJamesPublishing.com/giving-back

For those who are lost

TABLE OF CONTENTS

ACKNOWLEDGMENTS

Thank you to all of people who have helped me on this incredible journey: my parents, family, and friends, who are my greatest cheerleaders; Joyce Blaylock and John Boles, writing teachers, Mel Hughes, my editor and staunch supporter; Terry Whalin and all the wonderful staff at Morgan James Publishing.

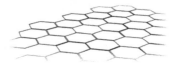

PART ONE

GUILT TRIP

I wake to shrill, repetitive blasts.

Hmmm. I have an alarm clock today.

It crashes to the ground as I fumble for the device in the darkness. The whole room moves at a different speed than me and my stomach lurches, warning me that last night's dinner is on its way up for breakfast. I fall from the bed, unsteadily rise to my feet, and stumble toward what I hope is the bathroom. The after-effects of biotransposition are in full force, and I barely make it over the toilet before what looks like falafel comes tumbling out. Hugging the porcelain stabilizes me until the spinning stops.

Once my faculties are under control, I straighten up and turn on the light. As is my usual course, I rinse my mouth out in the sink and look at what I am wearing. You can tell a lot about a person by their sleeping attire.

"What am I modeling this morning? Matching blue and gray pinstriped pajamas. Cotton. Ugh. I bet he color coordinates his sock drawer."

Lacking enthusiasm, I shuffle into the bedroom to find out who I will be today. My real name is Smullian, an unfortunate moniker given to me by my mother. Its origins have something to do with a pirate and a stolen barrel of Zevekan gin, but I digress. I'm a grifter by trade—that's a con man in your parlance. At least, I used to be a grifter until the coppers pinched me. The Powers-That-Be decided to sentence me to 1000 days Life Modification Therapy so that this humble criminal can "Learn the value of an honest day's labor and empathize with my victims." Simply stated, I'm a different person every day. In 776 days, all I've learned is that some people don't keep their bathrooms in logical places—there's no better way to start the day than mopping up vomit.

The closet causes further dismay. Golf shirts, all in muted colors, are arranged together followed by an inordinate number of khaki pants. At the back of the closet lurks suits, all navy. At least twenty shoe boxes sit on the floor.

"This guy keeps his shoes in the boxes, and I'm certain these hangers are equidistant from each other. He's either an accountant or a government employee—or worse, a government accountant. This guy never gets laid."

I am not looking forward to my day. If it were possible, I'd call in sick, but *They*, The Powers-that-Be, would know. I don't want any time added to my sentence.

"Keep your head down and your nose to the grindstone, Smullian my boy. One boring suit and an equally boring tie, comin' up."

To satisfy my curiosity and to cover his pedicured feet, I open the sock drawer. Sure enough, the navy ones are all neatly bundled on the left side of the drawer. The brown ones occupy the middle, and the athletic socks fill up the right. Unexpected, but not surprising, are three blue and white headbands.

"Tennis or jogging?"

I want to call my host something other than "This Guy," but his wallet is nowhere to be found. It's probably downstairs in one of those caddies by the front door along with his keys, cell phone, and some loose change.

Grifter 101 starts with reading a mark, and this guy screams, "Please, take me for everything I have." In another day and another time, I'd be able to play him like a violin. But, instead, I must embody him, this poor schlep that wouldn't know a good time if it went marching past him with blazing trumpets and bright orange pasties.

I'm not a bad guy. I have rules. I don't grift anyone who can't afford it or who doesn't deserve it. I provide a public service, teaching the population-at-large not to be as gullible as lemmings. Security consultants show corporations gaps in their defenses. I show people gaps in their financial planning. This one time I ran a scam raising money to save the endangered Quilla moths of Banta Five. Of course, Banta Five had been eaten up by a black hole three years earlier, but none of the schmucks bothered to do any research. I rolled it in hand over fist with that one. Financial Planning Lesson One: don't make decisions based on emotion. Or take the trouble to pick up an Astral Directory before contributing to a cause on a colony you've never heard of.

But I digress. Stepping away from the dresser, I give the room a once-over. Neat as a pin. Not surprising. Neutral colors and only a couple of wall hangings adorn the walls.

"Sheesh, would a little color kill this guy?"

Instead of a side table next to the bed, there's filing cabinet. A tasteful filing cabinet with highly polished dark wood and brass fittings, but it's a filing cabinet, nonetheless. It's position next to the bed means this guy's idea of settling down for a good night's sleep involves paperwork. I pull it open to peruse the files and see what other info I can glean about Joe Boring. The first tab says, "Pro Bono."

"Not only does he work in bed, but he does it for free," I mumble. "This guy is the worst. What kind of person gives away their skills and talents? A sucker, that's who."

I glance through the first folder and find out two things of value: this guy is in fact an accountant, and his name is Marvin Shoemacher.

"Marvin, really?"

I thumb through the rest of the file. They're all taxes. Most people consider filling out tax forms a form of torture, something to be avoided and postponed at all costs. Marvin does it for free. What a schmuck! I read through the names because names are part of the trade. I try to find identities for my alter egos that are a good blend of average and exotic. If a name's too bland, it seems fake. Too exotic, it sticks out. The files in the cabinet yield: Boles, not bad. Carter, how many of those in the known universe? Gondeck, a risk. Hawthorne—

"I am Father to the Fatherless," booms out of nowhere.

I jerk around fast, almost pulling a muscle in my back. "Who said that?"

The room is empty. The voice sounded like it was right on top of me, but no one stands there. Nothing in the room indicates a roommate. Haven't heard anything either. Roommates make noise. There hasn't been any grunts, bumps, or clanks. It is silent.

"I am Father to the Fatherless." Again, like there's a PA in here.

I hop up and do a check double check of the closet and bathroom. Empty. Dashing down the stairs, I perform a thorough search of what I now realize is a small condo. Even as I comb the space and try to process the strange voice, my mind notes that a condo makes perfect sense for our boy Marvin. It's practical and inexpensive. *His life motto, I'm sure.*

The hunt turns up no one. This could be some kind of bizarre practical joke, but Marvin doesn't seem like the kind of guy who'd have friends capable of imagining and perpetrating something like this—a disembodied voice uttering a senseless phrase. What would be the point? Plus, a prank on this level would require a recorder, hidden speakers, or maybe a wireless system. Regardless of the unlikelihood, I modify my search for hidden electronics. Again nothing. *Strange.*

"Who said that?" I demand, hoping the perpetrator will speak again and give me another clue. The house and the jokester are silent.

I go through the files to see if it happens again. Boles, Carter, Gondeck, Hawthorne, Phoenix. No disembodied voice.

"I bet this is related to Life Mod. They are projecting my consciousness across the centuries. Weird things could happen. Some kind of glitch. I wish I'd thought of this before I wasted time running around like galluden after a kwit."

This explanation satisfies me enough. I'm not one to worry over things that don't have a direct effect on my health and well-being. You can't survive as a grifter if you're a worrier. People can read anxiety, and, once they do, they're less likely to trust you with their hard-earned coin. I brush the incident away with the ease of a horse using his tail to swat a fly and get on with my boring day.

I predicted a caddy with Marvin's wallet, keys, and change would be by the front door. I am wrong; it's in the kitchen. The wallet tells me more about who I am for the day—Marvin Shoemacher of Jacksonville, Florida. His business card confirms he is an accountant and gives me his business address. The two hundred dollars cash nestled inside brightens me up. It saves me the time spent figuring out a pin code. Not that I can spend all of it; again, *They* monitor transactions. If *They* find spending is beyond what is "necessary for the due completion of the course of the host's conventional and logical daily activities," I get more time bouncing from person to person. It is my humble opinion that regurgitating every morning for 1000 days is punishment enough.

"Wheat germ extract and some kind of stinking protein shake," I mutter when I open the fridge. "Uh-uh, having to consume that would be cruel and unusual punishment. Marvin's arteries aren't going to harden in one day. I'm stopping at McD's."

You might be wondering how a simple grifter like me would be able do the "conventional and logical daily activities," of a 1000 different people. *The Exhaustive Lexicon of Twentieth and*

Twenty-First Century Labor Practices was downloaded onto a chip in my brain. However, I've found in my 776 days so far, it's not as exhaustive as we twenty-fourth centurians think. Yak herding, for example, is not in there (and milking one of those beasts is a lot harder than you might think). However, a job does not make a person. To replace a person, really be them, takes innate creativity and spontaneity, two qualities I possess in abundance. I will personify buttoned-down Marvin, and no one will be the wiser.

Along with the not-so-*Exhaustive Lexicon*, I was also downloaded with *Phraseology, Jargon, and Mores of Twenty-First Century Earth*. This is how I learned about things like McDonalds and Grande Fat-Free Frappuccinos, not that I drink them. A cold Coke in the morning goes a long way to soothing the after-effects of biotransposition.

They chose the twenty-first century because humans weren't yet using the full potential of their brains, making brain-hitching easy. Actual time travel is inaccurate and dangerous. You could be aiming for Detroit, Earth and end up on Detriate, a planet in the Aerial system—home of the largest lava sea in the universe. People in my century go to the past or the future by residing in the brains of someone living there already. Also, the tech on Earth in the 2000s is "sufficiently primitive to deter reprogramming of the Life Modification system." That's a prison break, in your jargon.

II

I print out a map to the address on Marvin's business card. GPS makes me nervous; you only have to get lost in Banjo Country one time to distrust that sweet voice telling you to turn left here. With the map tucked under my arm and his off-brand briefcase in my hand, I head out to the garage. That's when I see it. Next to the appropriately prim, green Volvo beckons something under a dust cover with curves in all the right places.

"What are you hiding under there, Marvin? Can I steal a little peek under the canvas?"

High gloss red shines in the dim light. Lust runs thick in my veins, and I must see the whole body. I rip off the canvas to reveal a sparkling, red Ferrari 599. While my instincts are to jump right in, I decide to take my time. This is an experience not to be rushed. I trail my hand along the pristine hood—no scratches, dents, or imperfections of any kind. My fingers follow this rise of her roof and, finally, dip down to her flawless trunk. Marvin keeps this baby in good shape. After a thorough examination of the exterior, I slide into the leather Recaro seat.

The interior sparkles as much as the exterior—polished dashboard, seats, and steering column. Just as I am beginning to question my first assessment of the man, I glance at the odometer. Even by twenty-first century standards, this car has gone nowhere.

I bet he's in here every Saturday, waxing and polishing, scrubbing the wheel covers with a toothbrush. But never takes her out. That's sadder than hanging out with a girl for years and never getting past first base. Poor Marvin, longing for adventure, but not taking the risk. He'd be the perfect mark for my Terrillian Safari Con, but alas, wrong time, wrong place.

The day, which started out dreadful, is on the rise. I get to drive one of the greatest sports cars ever created (I am talking centuries of contenders), and Marvin has a whole new layer that will make playing him loads of fun. The truth is, except for the daily retching and occasional yak herding, I enjoy Life Modification. This bid serves as *Advanced Training in the Art of the Con.* I get to hone my performance skills, expand my knowledge base, and learn more about the stupid things people do with their money.

The first genuine smile I've displayed since I was pinched dances on my face as I caress the Ferrari's steering wheel. My first love was a Toyota Ring Jumper T15 painted a look-at-me-yellow that shone like the sun. I was fourteen, and she was docked near a lake in a Junovian preserve, begging me to take her for a ride. I had already seen her owner, a prominent planetary official, sneak off into the bushes with a woman who was not his wife. I glanced around for possible witnesses. Finding none, I sauntered over for a closer look.

Her owner, in his rush, had failed to properly secure the cockpit hatch. At the time, I was working for a ring of chop shops.

They trained me in vehicle theft. I slid my skinny arm into the gap, opened her up, and scrambled inside. She was off the ground in no-time. The dope on the ground didn't even notice. Financial Planning Lesson Two—secure your assets. Or lock your vehicle before cheating on your wife.

Ring Jumpers do just that—they are capable of short orbit which is about the distance of a planet's rings. My heart almost stopped when I broke through atmo. By fourteen, I'd been to most of the planets in three galaxies, but always in big ships. This was new. The rush. The turbulence. I was hooked for life. Unfortunately, I wasn't that skilled a pilot and crashed her on an asteroid in Juno's fifth ring. I was fine, but forever changed.

This Ferrari makes me feel like I did when I was fourteen. I want to run, push her to her limits, and feel that power. I can be in Miami by lunch and the Keys by late afternoon. Fast car, fast women, good times.

But what about Marvin and his "conventional and logical daily activities?"

"Forget Marvin. *Neth*, the adventure would be good for him."

During brain-hitching, the host is placed in a subconscious state, a little like sleeping. He experiences everything the hitcher does, but events seem like dreams. When the hitcher is gone, the host has vague, fuzzy recollections, but remains convinced he was in full possession of his faculties. What if Marvin wakes to the sound of the pounding surf and the gentle breathing of some sexy brunette beside him? Maybe he will realize his dreams are possible and start living.

"I would be doing him a service. Now I have to go. It's a moral imperative."

I open the garage door and finger the ignition button. But what would The Powers-that-Be say? *They* will not be moved by the "It's best for Marvin," argument. *They* will say I was in violation of the terms and conditions of Life Modification Therapy. That I have left a host unduly and utterly stranded outside his natural environment, not to mention the "reasonable transactions" and "daily activities" clauses.

I wonder how much more time I would get. A week? I can handle a week. Ten days? It isn't ideal, but I could handle ten days. Who am I kidding? This would be thirty days minimum, and I'll only get off that light if they were sentencing a serial killer in the same docket. No, six months? A year? I sigh. Here I am on my 777th day, enduring my first ethical dilemma. I like Life Modification, but that doesn't mean I want to spend any more time in it than required. Is a day in this fine machine worth it?

I push the ignition and back down the driveway. With a final glance at my map, I head toward downtown.

"Man, Marvin's really starting to torque me off."

III

Traffic on San Jose is like driving in sludge, but I'm in the Ferrari. Even idling thrills in this car. I pass through an area of restored homes, kitschy boutiques, and trendy, certainly overpriced restaurants. The forced charm ends abruptly in a jangle of medical buildings, train tracks, and bridges. I ease past the congestion and find Marvin's building.

"Valet or self-serve?" Valet. I don't want to spend the evening trying to buff scratches out of Marvin's paint. After making sure the red baby is in good hands, I take the elevator up to the office.

Tanya, the secretary, emulates the Ferrari in human form. She has curves in all the right places and is bright red—from her red pumps to her matching wrap-around dress to her vibrantly dyed hair. He hired her for the same reason he bought the car—longing. *I wonder how many hours he's wasted, wishing he could wax and polish her.*

As the day progresses, I am pleasantly surprised to find that there is a fine brain underneath all that hair dye. Tanya is efficient, professional, and a skilled bookkeeper in her own right. Marvin is too practical to hire a secretary for looks alone. Without her to distract me, I'd have plunged a pencil into my eye by now. I despise numbers; I'm good with them but hate them just the same.

As soon as the clock rolls to 12:00, I jump out of my seat.

"Ready for lunch?" I ask.

Tanya looks at me with wide eyes. "Lunch?"

Smullian, you idiot. Marvin eats at his desk, probably something with tofu and sprouts. He doesn't eat out, and he never asks Tanya. While *They* wouldn't punish me for this little blunder, I mentally berate myself for acting like an amateur. I look around my desk for a way to explain this behavior. My eyes land on an envelope, and I stammer, "To celebrate the Goodman account."

"Oh," Tanya responds, her lipsticked mouth a red circle and an equally red blush hitting her cheeks. "Sure, I'll set the machine."

A demure smile touches her lips as she rushes about the office. Blunder or not, it is clear lunch out appeals to her. Maybe Marvin could have a shot if he'd pull his head out of the clouds. We ride in the elevator for several awkward moments (Marvin would have no idea what to say) and walk to the garage.

A cop questions the valet. "I hope no one's hurt," Tanya says.

The valet looks up at me and his tan face fades to white. "I was just about to call you, sir."

"Call me?"

The cop turns and looks at me, "Are you the owner of a 2007 red Ferrari 599 license plate NUMBRS?"

"Yes," I answer, drawing out the word until it sounds like a hiss.

"I regret to inform you that your vehicle has been stolen."

I've only biotransposed once while awake. I was a DJ in LA. Late party, late after-hours party, you get the hint. Not that I was geeked out, mind you. I learned to party clean the hard way. I fell afoul of some oversynthed jawa (twenty-fourth century speed). One guy died from it; I just got so sick I vowed to avoid all chemicals. Anyway, I'm making out with this over-bleached blonde when I feel like someone has grabbed my intestines and jerked them out through my nose. Just about the time I thought my head was going to explode, I found myself blowing chunks over the side of a Japanese whaler. That experience pales in comparison to how I feel when Johnny Law utters those words.

I wonder, for a moment, if a cicada has taken up residence in my ear. A high-pitched buzzing drowns out all communication around me. Dudley Do Right is saying something, but I can't hear it. Someone has stolen my car. Technically it is Marvin's car, but today it's my baby and someone nicked it! I am flummoxed, flabbergasted, and freaked out. What did I do to deserve this?

Maybe that's not the best question to ask.

Before I can ruminate on the answer, a soft hand lands on my arm, neutralizes the buzzing, and brings my mind into focus. "Marvin, he asked if you have Lojak," Tanya says.

Of course, Buttoned-down Marvin has Lojak. I am also sure he has the extended warranty and insurance on his floor mats. I am beginning to appreciate his anal, er, cautious nature.

"Yes," I answer, relief pouring out of me. "I have Lojak." The copper makes a call to initiate it and soon my baby is being tracked by satellite. We determine, based on the inept valet's statement, a classic diversion-and-grab was used. An underdressed, surgically-endowed broad occupied the valet by asking for directions. While Rocks for Brains was keeping his eyes in front, if you know what I mean, someone slipped in and grabbed the keys. *This doofus was taken by one of the oldest gaffes in the book.* Financial Planning Lesson Three—Thoroughly vet all business associates or don't hand your car keys to a hormone-besotted valet.

It's all over but the shouting. I need to go home, gather the Ferrari's papers, and take them to the station—like I want to spend my afternoon in a cop shop. I'm allergic to bad lighting and Formica.

Tanya drives me home in her perky, clean Volkswagen Beetle. I take one look at the spotless interior and know, beyond the shadow of a doubt, she is the girl for Marvin. However, I am too annoyed to do anything about it. Not annoyed, angry. I am angry with Tanya for being so understanding. I am angry with the valet for having a distinct lack of self-control. I am angry with myself for trusting the dolt. *Drak*, I'm angry with Marvin for buying the stupid car in the first place.

I fume silently while Tanya tries to make conversation. I only speak to give her directions, and those words are hardly more than grunts. As much as I try to deflect my feelings onto those other things, the truth lurks in my mind, and I can't deny it. I am a victim. Me—the victim of a con. Albeit through twisted and confusing circumstances, the fact remains the same. I feel helpless and violated. My stomach rolls like the time I entered a chili eating competition, and, for some bizarre reason, I itch all over.

That uncomfortable question comes back to me: *What did I do to deserve this?*

I've done plenty to deserve this, but today I am Marvin, and Marvin has done nothing. Just that morning I'd said he was screaming to be taken for everything he had. That was the morning, now I know him better. The dull schmuck works his posterior off to earn that car; he sacrifices and saves, obeys the law, and watches his cholesterol. Marvin does not deserve to have the fruits of his labor stolen from him. There is no way to rationalize it.

It gets worse. I helped. The car wouldn't have been stolen if I'd left it in the garage where Marvin wanted it. The itchiness increases, and my chest tightens. Tanya reaches my house, and I explode from the car. I just stalk inside without a wave goodbye. Being a mover, I can't think sitting still. Once my legs are pumping, clean air fills my lungs.

"Calm down, Smullian my boy. This is what *They* want." The light bulb dings in my brain, and I immediately feel better. *They* want me to "learn the value of an honest day's labor and empathize with my victims." I almost fell for it. *They* can't engineer a car theft (it was truly chance), but it's the kind of thing The Powers-that-Be have based their whole system on. "Prolonged exposure to law-abiding and virtuous citizens will, by necessity, alter an aberrant mindset." In short, leave a crook in Life Mod long enough, and he'll change his wicked ways.

Well, not this one. Besides I'm not a bad guy; I have rules. I don't grift anyone who can't afford it or who doesn't deserve it. Marvin may not deserve it, but he can afford it. I am betting he is more than amply insured. A quick perusal through his files proves my hypothesis. I smile to myself as I collect the paperwork the boy in blue had requested. Everything is back in perspective. Marvin will either get his car back or enough money to buy a new one. "Whew. No skin off my nose. Moral crisis averted."

The itch leaves, my heart rate normalizes, and the jaunt is back in my step. I even hum a spirited Galwan tune. Galwa is a charming backwater sphere on the wrong side of the universe's tracks and home to yours truly. It doesn't have a lot to offer—farming's difficult and there's limited natural resources. Most people work in the salt mines. Some industrious types, like me and my mom, find more creative forms of finance. Mom milked the My Baby Needs Medicine scam when I was only a month old. But I digress.

IV

Marvin's Volvo takes me to the cop shop in a safe and efficient manner, as advertised. Once there, I commence my favorite pastime—waiting. As I already said, I'm not one for sitting still. It's unnatural. Internally we're in constant motion: blood is pumping, neurons are firing, glands are producing all kinds of fluids, yet we think it's possible to rein in all that movement and be still. I want to fidget, pace, talk, but I know Buttoned-up Marvin is a sitter. He'd be patiently staring into space holding his documents. So, I muster up all my will power (which isn't much, mind you) and do the same.

When I think I'll explode from all the excess energy, I quietly rise and shuffle to the water fountain. This is a pretty high-tech cop shop; they have the kind with cups instead of the usual bubbler. I pour myself a drink and nurse it while reading the safety notices on the wall. There is a bulletin for the elderly about phone charity scams. I study it to see if there are any I can modify for my own purposes. Charity scams are a cash crop, but I have rules. I wouldn't scam an old person, you know, unless they were rich.

Next to me a Latino detective who looks a little like Benjamin Bratt is talking to a waitress. He sports a suit—not blues—affirming his rank. Her powder-blue retro diner uniform skirt ends just above her mannequin perfect calves. I can't see her face but, who cares, with legs like that?

I pick up scraps of their conversation. "He wouldn't skip school," she says.

"I understand that, ma'am, but a lot of kids do. I'm sure he'll come home later with a perfect explanation," Benjamin Bratt says.

"No. He wouldn't go off without telling me. You have to look for him."

"Ma'am, he's fifteen. We can't file a report until he's been gone 24 hours. Go home and—"

"I am Father to the Fatherless," someone whispers behind me. *Again?* I glance around and see no one. Only Benjamin Bratt, Lovely Legs, and I. *Must be a strange trick of the acoustics.* "I am Father to the Fatherless." It utters right next to me. The detective and waitress continue their conversation; they haven't heard it. The phrase seems directed at me, like it's somehow a description and a command at the same time. I haven't experienced auditory hallucinations before, but anything is possible in Life Mod. I mean they've taken my essence and crammed it into some dude's brain three centuries in my past. Weird stuff is bound to happen. I handle it the way I do all things I don't understand—I walk away. After an unobtrusive saunter around the lobby, I take my seat.

It isn't long before a tired-looking detective approaches. "Mr. Shoemacher?" he asks.

I jump up and eagerly hand him my folder. "I've brought all the documents you asked for." In perfect Marvin form, I open it and began to explain, "Here's my title, and this is the insurance policy, and here's—"

"Mr. Shoemacher, that's all very helpful," he interrupts. Judging from the bags under his eyes, it's been a long day. Eager beaver Marvin annoys him. "However, it won't be necessary. We've recovered your vehicle. Can you step out back with me to the impound lot and ID it?"

My car! I'll be able to drive that baby home and put her under her dust cover just the way Marvin likes it. When I biotranspose, all will be right in Marvin's world. I follow Grumpy out to the lot and there she is, just as promised. I inspect her closely, searching for the slightest damage. I find not a knick, mark, or scratch. This little bump in the road is almost over.

Detective Needs-A-Personality takes me back in, where I fill out and sign forms until my hand cramps. When he says I am done, I ask him for the keys.

"The Ferrari 599 is evidence. It will be some time before you can take it home," he says as casually as if he's asking me if I want fries with that.

"Didn't you catch the thief in the act?"

"Yes, but there's still processing."

Man, this day really sucks. I'm a grifter; I am well acquainted with processing. Marvin is not, so I keep up the charade. "What kind of processing? How long will that take?"

"Processing," he repeats with a bland expression. "Shouldn't take more than two, three days. We'll call."

Two or three days would be an eternity to Marvin. I start to get that itchy feeling again, and I don't like it. Which is why I do what I do next, for the sole purpose of throwing Marvin a bone (in a manner of speaking), I call Tanya. Her number is right there in his phone.

"Hello," she says.

"Hello, Tanya, this is Marvin Shoemacher from work." He'd maintain professionalism.

"I know who you are, Marvin," she says, giggling. It isn't a mocking giggle. It is more of a You're-So-Cute giggle.

Encouraged that my assumptions are correct, I continue. "I'm sorry our celebration lunch got canceled this afternoon."

"Me too."

"I was wondering, if you don't have other plans, if we could reschedule for tomorrow noon?"

"That would be great," she gushes.

"All right, then. Lunch, noon tomorrow. I'll see you at work in the morning," I finish, hanging up the phone. *There, I have led my horse to water. I wonder if he'll drink.* I drive home, collapse on the couch, and will myself to sleep. Being Marvin is way too stressful—I am ready to be someone new.

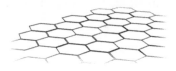

PART TWO

BETTER LIVING THROUGH DENIAL

The pumping, rhythmic tones of Latin rap wake me, limiting the options of where I am to only half the entire planet. The room spins more than usual, and I am contemplating whether it is wise to stay where I am or try to move when something warm snuggles against my back. I hold out hope that it's a wet-nosed dog until a lilting, sleepy voice says, "Turn it off, querido."

That makes my decision. I am off the bed and into the bathroom faster than a Ring Jumper. I barely have time to lock the door behind me before this guy's dinner comes to call. *A significant other!* Significant others are trouble. A wife or girlfriend knows the host better than anyone, and she's there the moment I wake up in his body. I don't have a chance to investigate his personality before I have to put on a show. This is the only situation where I'm glad for my morning caller. Any behavior she suspects, I can deflect with, "I think I caught whatever's going around."

The door handle jiggles, and I am glad I remembered to lock it. Life Mod detainees always brainhitch in their gender. It's hard enough navigating a new person without also having to convince others you're the opposite sex. However, a clever quirk in the system is that I rarely have a wife. Usually I am a bachelor, widower, or someone too young to be bothered. However rare, it became clear early on that I needed to lock the door. Wives will follow their sick husbands into the bathroom to pat their backs and cool their fevered brows.

On one awkward occasion, a girlfriend followed me into the shower. Most guys would think *easy money* in that situation. The ultimate hook-up, no strings attached. Not me. I have rules. I never touch a married woman. Marriage is a sacred institution that should be respected by all parties, inside or out. A concept my father had trouble wrapping his alcohol-addled brain around.

The handle jiggles again. A delicate knock follows. "Are you okay, querido?"

I am still somewhat busy over the throne, but I manage, "un minuto." It confounds me that my brain and its language chip are three centuries away, and yet I know what it knows. How do the techies manage that? I don't even pause. I just know what to say. Too bad *They* remove the chip when my sentence is over. *Ah, the trouble I could get into.*

"Okay," the wife answers, and I assume (hope) she leaves. After I finish, I realize she spoke in both Spanish and halting English. Like she was just learning, but it was English, nonetheless. *Am I in the US again?* It is rare, but not unheard of, to be in the same country two days in a row.

I turn on the faucet and rummage through the medicine cabinet. I need info and fast. Most of the stuff in there is generic. I do find out my guy likes his cologne. There must be five different designer scents. That combined with his red bikini briefs tells me this guy is one step short of a metrosexual.

Under the sink I find all her things: hair gel, blow dryer, barrettes, bobby pins, facial cleansers, but very little make-up. *She's a natural beauty. There was no way Cologne Man has an ugly chick. Jackpot!* Along with everything else is a prescription bottle, antibiotics of some kind. Her name is Marisol Diaz. Having her name is more important than his at this moment. Women are funny, they only put up with being called Doll, Baby, Querida so long before they expect to hear their name.

I glance at the pharmacy address to find out my city. I am guessing I am in the southwest. *Arizona, New Mexico?* I haven't been those places yet. *Jacksonville, FL.* I freeze. To be in the same city is unheard of. In fact, *They* have a clause about it. "In order to maximize cultural exposure and minimize exposure of Life Modification Therapy, candidates will inhabit hosts of differing cities on a daily basis." In other words, they don't want you crossing paths with your previous host. It's not like sci fi of the twenty-first century, there won't be a matter-antimatter explosion or a time paradox. *They* are worried there will be recognition on a subconscious level. That recognition could lead to speculation which would be bad for the system.

On top of being in the same city, I am in the same area of town. Jacksonville is huge. Not Balspar huge, a city that covers a planet with the same name. However, by most standards, Jax spans a lot of land. I learned as Marvin that living in two different parts of town could be like living in a different city. But I drove down that pharmacy's street yesterday.

I drop the bottle and look in the mirror at myself. No wonder my guy is metrosexual, he is handsome. Movie star handsome, Benjamin Bratt handsome. I examine the face in the mirror and picture him in a suit. I know him. He was the detective talking to Lovely Legs in the cop shop lobby yesterday. Not only am I in the same area of the same city, I am someone I had been in contact with the day before.

"Oh boy, there is something seriously wrong with Life Mod."

I inspect the glitch from every angle. As far as I know, it started the day before with the weird voice saying, "I am Father to the Fatherless." I heard it when I was near Marvin's filing cabinet, and when I was standing near the guy who's my current brain-hitching host. If the voice was a system hiccup, the first time the only nearby human was *occupado* with me. But the second time, Pretty Boy was nearby—maybe the code reset on him. He didn't have a hitcher and was available, so to speak. *Makes sense, sort of. Anyhow, it isn't my problem. They have messed up, and They will have to fix it.*

I flash a grin at my new self in the mirror and say, "There's no way they can pin this on you, you handsome devil." I need to do what I do every day. Put my nose to the grindstone and stay out of trouble. No Ferraris for me, no sir. I will do it all by the book, which is longer than *War and Peace*. Detainees applying for Life Mod must read *Acceptable Conduct and Behavior for Life Modification Therapy*. It is time to get on with Pretty Boy's "conventional and logical daily activities."

There is still the matter of Marisol, the wife, to contend with. I decide to implement part one of my Wife Exit Strategy. Simply stated—get out of the house as quickly as possible. Luckily, I already know this guy's job and where he works. All I have to do is get dressed, grab the keys, and skedaddle.

Pretty Boy's closet is far more promising than Marvin's had been. Benjamin Bratt has taste. Nothing designer, he couldn't afford that on a cop's salary, but good quality, nonetheless. He also isn't afraid of color, like most guys. He has every hue in the rainbow represented. However, his work suits are appropriately sedate. I grab a dark blue one and accent it with a bright red and yellow silk tie. I would go with a milder one, but he doesn't have any.

It is clear Marisol has similar taste. Her side of the closet is equally bright although she has far more casual clothes than Pretty Boy. I bet she stays at home. But why? Kids? I don't hear any shrieking.

I snatch Pretty Boy's wallet off the dresser and glance at his driver's license. Benigno Diaz. *Cool, now I have a name.* His badge is next to the wallet, so I clip it on my belt. I open the door and start down the hall when I remember his service revolver. He's supposed to have it with him 24/7. I wonder where he keeps it when he sleeps. Benigno is serious about his clothes, I am sure he is also serious about his job. He'd keep his gun near him at all times. Bedside table? Most logical spot. *Please, please, please be in a thumbprint safe. I do not have the time or energy to finesse a four-digit pin out of Marisol.*

I pull the table door open and find the safe, as predicted. *Yes! Thumbprint.* I place Benny Boy's digit on the pad. A muffled ka-chunk sounds the lock's release. I turn the handle, and the door swings open, revealing its lethal occupant. I don't want to pick it up; I know how to use it, sure. My chip has all sorts of information, but I've never actually held one. Technology in my day may be more advanced, but a weapon is a weapon. People still get hurt by them. I use my gift for gab to get me out of tight spots, I don't need anything else. Still, it's part of Benigno's "conventional and logical daily activities" to carry it with him. I settle the holster and its charge under my jacket. I've heard guys say that guns make them feel powerful; I just feel off-balance.

As I trot down the stairs, I notice that Benny was also serious about his heritage. All the furnishings are of Latin influence along with the art on the walls. I recognize a colorful rendition of La Perla from my day as a tour guide in San Juan. *Benny Boy must be Puerto Rican.* I am almost out the door when I am interrupted.

"Benigno," Marisol says from behind me. I whirl around and notice three things. First, she is holding a plate with toast and a glass with some clear liquid. Sprite or 7-up? Second, she is, in fact, a natural beauty. Her dark, wavy hair falls loosely around her shoulders, framing her face and equally dark almond-shaped eyes. Third, she is exploding with baby. *Man, I don't need this today. What if I get shot? Why do I gotta have the responsibility for leaving little Pedro without a daddy? They better get this glitch fixed fast. I don't think I can spend the day in RIOT gear.*

"*Coma para su estomago*," she says, concern lacing her 86% cacao eyes. Translation: Eat for your stomach. *Great, she's trying to take care of me.* My options don't look good. I can blow her off, saying I am fine, and risk hurting her overly sensitive pregnant wife feelings. Or I can stay and eat, pleasing the little woman, but increasing the risk of raising her suspicions.

I smile warmly and kiss her on the cheek, picking up notes of coconut. *Her shampoo or is it lotion?* I say in Spanish, "You're too good to me, sweetheart. I'm much better." Taking the drink from her hand, I add, "I'll drink this in the car. Don't wait up—we have a lot of cases." Part two of Wife Exit Strategy—work as late as possible. She kisses me back, and I escape.

As I drive to the cop shop, drinking my Sprite/7-Up, which does help my somersaulting stomach, I ruminate on the situation. I'm not a marrying kind of man. Heck, I'm not even a monogamous kind of man. I'm a different girl, different planet every night kind of guy. I don't want the responsibility of another person's health, wealth, and happiness weighing on my shoulders. And I certainly don't want my health, wealth, and happiness to be dependent on someone else. It's a slippery slope. People always leave.

I think about Benigno, his wife, and their bun in the oven. He has a potentially dangerous job. How can he go to work each day, knowing those lives depend on him? I pause. It's day 778, and I've never been in a host with a death-defying job. I was a sports mascot (Go Wolverines!) but I don't think that counts.

While there isn't a clause about dangerous work that I can remember, there is "the candidate will not participate in any activity that could potentially threaten the livelihood and physical well-being of his host." Getting shot by a crack addict would certainly threaten Benigno's livelihood and physical well-being. I realize that I need to be extra careful today. When *They* review the glitch, my behavior should be stellar. I park in the lot and make my way inside.

II

Being in the cop shop again is eerie. Life Mod drops me in a different person in a different location every day. I haven't experienced déjà vu since back in the twenty-fourth century; nothing has seemed familiar for more than two years. So being in this place where I've walked and talked with people is more than a little off-putting. I know the guy behind the desk and can recite the poster about charity scams.

I haven't felt this edgy since the last time I was on Earth. Me and Cod, a man who smelled like his name, were pulling Good Samaritan jobs. I prefer to work alone, but those scams require two people. Anyway, Cod got himself caught. I watched the oinkers nab him, cuff him, and haul him away. I imagined a giant blinking red arrow over my head saying, "Con man, arrest, arrest."

I spent the rest of the day looking behind me more than I looked forward. Of course, my suspicion was warranted because Cod rolled over for the boys in blue, and I got pinched. Further proof that you can't rely on other people; they betray you. That's when I ended up in Life Mod. I hope *this* day, with its major system glitch, won't have equally disastrous outcomes.

Steady, Smullian my boy. Today is just another day. Nose to the grindstone.

Based on my guy's conversation with Lovely Legs, I figure Beningno reports to Missing Persons. After a quick scan of the directory, I make my way to the third floor. Very few people wander around the space, which is good because I need time to find his desk. The search takes a few minutes. Benny Boy's desk doesn't need a name plaque—the framed picture of Marisol identifies the sappy user. Sitting next to the phone is my first case of the day. The irony of a grifter solving any kind of crime isn't lost on me.

A secretary had called to report her boss, Robert R. Clausen, as missing. I know he's up to something. Everyone knows that Bobs and Bobbys are great guys. Men who insist on Robert are shifty. And don't get me started on Robs. But I digress.

Unable to contact him for three days, she had gone by his house this morning, only to find no one at home. Hmm. Going by the house rates a little more than regular secretary duties. I wonder if they had more than a "working" relationship. Poor Melinda, she must not know the Rob/Robert rule. It is possible she's in on it, whatever *it* is. Only one way to find out. I pick up the phone and dial her number.

Melinda confirms Robert's malfeasance, of which she is unaware. Her distress and confusion are evident. "Something bad must have happened to him," she says. "Otherwise, Robert would have called me." She believes this relationship exists beyond steaming up the storage closet. Unfortunately, her only crime is having deplorable judgment in men.

Then she says something that sets off all my bells and whistles. "On top of everything else, my check wasn't in my account this morning."

"You have direct deposit?" I ask calmly. I bet Robert cleared out the accounts and escaped to the Caymans.

"Yes, I thought maybe there was an error at the bank. So, I called, but they said if there was an error it wasn't on their end." Doubt creeps into her tone. She is starting to wonder if he had, in fact, left her. She is starting to wonder if he is capable of pilfering the payroll. She is putting it together.

"We'll find him." *In line at Jax International clutching his passport.* "I'll keep you apprised of the situation."

"Thank you," she says. "He would call me, I know it." *Now, who's she trying to convince?*

There are two avenues to pursue here—the missing man and the missing money. I'm lazy. Grifting requires little work on my part, due to my natural talent. A good haul supports my lavish (if you call eating three times a day lavish) lifestyle for three or four months. No one will ever accuse me of going the extra mile. I am delighted when I realize the money is not my problem. Making a quick call to Economic Crime, I hand that part off to someone named Fuller.

That leaves me the missing man. Before I can get embroiled in it, another detective with a buzz cut parks himself on my desk. Something about his wide smile and square jaw says "high school quarterback" to me.

"What have we got today, Benny?" he asks.

Partner? Another first. I've been so busy worrying about the wife; I haven't stopped to consider the possible ramifications of the rest of the day. The way I figure it, partners could be just as bad as wives, depending on how long they've been working with my host.

"You're late," I say, stalling.

"Only by fifteen minutes," he answers with a Super Bowl-sized grin.

I take a risk based on what little I knew about Benny, a man serious enough about his heritage to speak Spanish at home and hang ethnic art on his walls.

"And my name's Benigno. How many times do I have to tell you that?"

"At least twice a day, Benny boy." He chuckles and slaps me on the shoulder. "What's new?"

I fill him in on Robert, and the steps I'd taken thus far. "I was about to fax his info to airport and railroad security."

"I'll get Miller to run over to Greyhound. He's eager. Let him spend the morning at the bus terminal talking with the jewels of Jacksonville society."

I like the partner, whatever his name is. He doesn't take life too seriously—my kind of guy. I could be friends with a guy like him, if I was in the habit of making friends. I watch my partner amble off to tell Miller he would be spending the morning in a dank bus station with homeless people and diesel fumes. When he is gone, I shuffle through some old reports on my desk to find his name. Charles Weidman. *This guy goes by Charlie—that much I know.* I watch him joke around with Miller and another cop.

Cheshire Charlie might be a problem. I don't have the luxury of taking off as I did with Marisol that morning; I'll be stuck with him all day. My only advantage is his Y chromosome. Guys, by nature, aren't as observant as women. Still, I need to have a plan for dealing with him. Bringing up the whole I'm-not-feeling-myself thing becomes priority one.

I fax the info about Robert to the appropriate agencies and walk to the kitchenette. It's stocked with coffee, tea, and an assortment of the finest innovations of the twentieth century—Krispy Kreme donuts. You'd think with all the technology we have in my time we'd be able to make a decent donut, but alas, that skill has gone the way of spinning and weaving. I can almost feel the confection melting in my mouth. With a sigh of frustration, I grab a plain bagel.

"Didn't Marisol make you a four-course breakfast?" Charlie asks from behind me.

"My stomach was off this morning. I think I caught whatever's going around. Her mallorca bread and eggs are much better than this," I say, waving the bagel in the air.

"Thompson from Records was bent over the toilet in the men's room this morning."

"How long did he spend at Happy Hour last night?" I ask with a conspiratorial grin.

"Good question, Benny."

"Benigno."

Charlie blows off my statement with a chuckle, something I have a feeling he does often. "There's someone asking for you. Wasn't she here yesterday?"

I've been to most of the planets in the known universe. I've played chess with a giant gastropod, that's a slug to the undereducated, who smoked and moved the pieces around with his antennae. I once discussed the works of Aldis Hexter, a twenty-second century prose poet, with a rock who had great insight into the symbolism. I know weird. Seeing was not required for believing who sat at my desk. Only one person could complete the orbit of odd I am circling in—Lovely Legs.

"You know the one," Charlie continued. "The waitress with the nice stems."

III

I walk to my desk with Charlie hot on my heels. I have a feeling he isn't overly concerned about the particulars of the case itself, but rather putting himself in the position of being Lovely Legs' hero. I run over the bit of conversation I'd overheard the day before: skipped school, fifteen, twenty-four hours—got it, should be enough to bluster through the intake interview.

Even from a distance, I can tell she isn't old enough to have a fifteen-year-old. Unless she'd had him when she was seven and that's only possible on Tarnis where the people age and mature at a highly accelerated rate. A Tarnian will live an entire lifetime in twenty years, it's quite amazing. This makes them great marks because they don't have the experience and wisdom of races with longer life spans. A Tarnian will fall for a Three Dige Shuffle (twenty-fourth century Three Card Monte) over and over and over again. I always head to Tarnis when pickin's are slim everywhere else.

Back to Lovely Legs. Why is she reporting this kid missing and not his parents? Interesting. She is wearing jeans, which means she was taking the day off, not that I blame her. I miss the waitress uniform, though. My mind flutters back to an image of her perfect hourglass figure and sculpted legs. Based on that memory, I have great hopes for her face. Those hopes, however, are utterly dashed with one glance.

She's probably been crying for the last twenty hours. Red splotches cover her cheeks. Her nose is swollen to what must be twice its normal size and crusty stuff rings the nostrils. The red in her eyes makes the blue of her irises glow with an unearthly intensity. She looks like a plague victim— or a heroin addict going through withdrawal.

Charlie takes a detour and heads for his desk. I understand why; I'd do it too in his position. He isn't required to be there. I am. Mind you, he didn't take off because she looked hideous. He left for his own safety. A woman's tears are a man's kryptonite. We are powerless in their sway. When exposed to them, we find ourselves compelled to do anything, everything to make them stop. We, normally rational and logical beings, will behave in manners beyond comprehension to end the torrent. There is nothing more dangerous than a woman who understands this power. However, Lovely Legs is not manipulating. The throes of pure grief envelop her. *This is the last place I want to be.*

I try to distance myself by fumbling around my desk for the intake form. I open a drawer and paw past a stapler, several sharpened pencils, and a beat-up copy of *Devotions for Police Officers*. I close it and open another drawer; it has neatly labeled files. "Intake Form," reads the fourth label. I clear my throat a couple of times and steel my willpower. *You're only a hitcher, Smullian. Here today, gone tomorrow. This is not your problem.*

"Your name?" I ask, keeping my eyes locked on the form in front of me.

"Lydia Hawthorne."

"Age?"

"Twenty-one."

I continue until I have all the spaces, boxes, and lines filled in. The victim is David Hawthorne, fifteen. Missing for one day. I know all about police procedure from the chip, but there isn't any information about how to conduct an interview. Grifter policy is to let the mark blather on and on. The more they talk, the more useful info you get. The most inconsequential tidbit can be a goldmine in the hands of a master. I figure it is the same for a cop. So, I lay down my pen and shift my chair to face her. Looking her in the eyes, I say, "Tell me what happened."

Lydia fiddles with the book she clutches in her lap. "I worked a double, night before last. I got home after he went to bed. At least, I think he was in bed. I didn't actually see him; the door was shut and the light was off. I don't normally work doubles. I don't like him to be home alone, but we've been saving up for *Rock the Universe* this weekend. It was a chance to make a little more for our trip."

Rock the Universe?

She keeps rambling, "David wants to see Skillet, and I've been dying to see Toby Mac. I hear he's really good live."

Ah, a concert of some sort.

"We got our tickets a while back, but there's hotel, food, gas, souvenirs. We've been saving for months. David did odd jobs for Mrs. Granger, our neighbor, all summer—changing light bulbs, taking out her trash, carrying her groceries. She's eighty- something. We've both worked hard for this trip. It's supposed to be our first one together since—" New tears splash over her lower lids and down her cheeks. She fiddles with the book in her lap some more, tracing the edges with her fingers over and over. She pauses so long I am about to prompt her, when she looks up, tears gone, and continues.

"Our parents died last November. Mom, Dad, and Jesse, our brother, were driving back from an away game in Chattanooga. Jesse's soccer team was undefeated. Another car lost control on Monteagle and forced them into the rocks. Mom and Dad died instantly. Jesse held on for a couple of days, but he didn't make it.

"David hadn't gone with them. He'd stayed at a friend's house that day. I was down here going to UNF, so it made sense for David to move here from Nashville. Going to school and taking care of him was too much. I dropped out and started working at the diner. We couldn't afford to keep the house in Nashville, so we sold it." A gentle smile touches her lips. It is the first glimmer I see of the beauty she has on better days. "In this market, we were very blessed to find a buyer quickly. I put the money aside for David's college."

I'd have used that money to get my butt out of the diner. What twenty-one- year-old puts a huge chunk of change in savings—for someone else?

"David had it hard for a long time. I guess kind of a survivor's guilt. He felt like he should have been there. That he'd been selfish not to go to Jesse's game. I told him it was a blessing. Otherwise, I'd be all alone. He started getting better over the summer. He was excited about the new school year. That's how I know he didn't skip. He liked school.

"When I went to work yesterday morning, he wasn't up yet. When I got home from my shift, he wasn't there. His backpack wasn't there either—and no note. There was a message in my voicemail from the school saying he'd been absent. He wouldn't take off somewhere without telling me. He wouldn't do that to me. He knows I'd worry. The last time I saw him was two days ago. I went in later than usual that morning because of the double. I made him pancakes." She finishes, reaching across the desk toward me. Her eyes fix on mine, doing their own quiet pleading as tears renew the tracks down her face. "You have to find him."

Strength failing, kryptonite working. Keep it together, Smullian.

I break her gaze and try to maintain a business-like composure. "What about Mrs. Granger?" I ask. "Did you ask her if she'd seen him?"

"She said she thought she heard him leaving yesterday morning."

Note: Check with old lady.

"What about his friends? Did you call them?"

"He doesn't really have any yet. As I said, it's taken him some time to come out of his shell."

No friends she knows about. Note: Check with school.

I hate to say it, but there is a real possibility he's run away. He sounds like a textbook case. It's a gift of people in my trade to suggest something, but make the mark think it was their idea. I use my skills to make the harsh question come from her.

"A move like that can be hard at his age. He must miss his friends in Nashville a great deal."

"He Facebooks them from the library. I had to drop the smart phone. I couldn't afford the bill. I just use a pay as you go flip phone. He doesn't get to talk to them as much as he'd like."

I remember that she'd said the concert would be their first trip. Based on that, I set the hook. "Have you two gone back to see any of them since the move?"

"No, he hasn't seen his friends in almost a year." A strange expression cascades over her face, her hand flies to her mouth. "Did he go home?" she asks, more to herself than me. She sits like that for a moment, her hand frozen where it is, her eyes drifting back and forth. She is thinking it through. I am thankful I didn't have to suggest it.

Then she drops her hand to my desk, straightens her back, and sets her jaw. "No," she says with a rapid shake of her head. "No, he wouldn't do that to me. He wouldn't go off without telling me." She punctuates the last two words by jabbing my desk with an emphatic forefinger. She shakes her head again. "He knows I'd worry. Something's happened and you need to find out what," she finishes, pointing the same finger at my chest. The crumpled girl is gone; this woman is feisty, and I admire her. I figure this display of spunkiness was closer to her true personality. This woman would take on raising a teenager without a second thought. She is a survivor.

If you watch a show like *Star Trek*, you'd get the idea that situations like this don't happen in the future. That there's some utopian government taking care of young girls forced to raise their little brothers. What a joke. Think about it, if people like Lydia fall through the cracks in a place as small as the United States, how many must fall through the cracks in a place as large as the known universe? That imagined utopian government of the future is really a bunch of committees and subcommittees arguing about border disputes and mining rights. People in need are left to make their own way. With Dad in and out, my mom and me had to find creative forms of finance. I already told you she was working the My-Baby-Needs-Medicine scam when I was only a month old. Actually, I might have needed medicine, but you get the point.

What about Lydia? The case makes me feel bad in the pit of my stomach, and it isn't just because of her kryptonite tears. Every way I look at the situation, it is drakked and the outcome isn't going to be happy. Either David ran away, which means that Lydia's only surviving family member has betrayed her, or something bad has happened to him and, come on, hasn't she seen enough tragedy?

Con men succeed because they can rationalize everything they do. A really good one can rob a blind cripple and convince you it was the right thing. My own rules keep my conscience clear. I don't grift anyone who can't afford it or who doesn't deserve it. Those principles have gotten me through 777 days of Life Mod unscathed. I don't feel bad for Melinda, the secretary whose boss took advantage of her. She should have known all that *overtime* would come to no good. Yesterday, Marvin could afford to have his Ferrari stolen. Financially, the theft would have been a small bump in the road. In either case, those schlubs created their own problems.

I can't rationalize Lydia. There is nothing to play on. I don't want this to be my responsibility, even for just a day. I think briefly about taking the entire squad room hostage and screaming that

I am being invaded by a body snatcher. If I did that, The Powers That Be would yank me out of Benigno faster than a galluden after a kwit. According to *Acceptable Conduct and Behavior of Life Modification Candidates,* "Any act which exposes the integrity of Life Modification Therapy will render the candidate's therapy null and void. Said candidate will be returned to his body for alternative punishment." Personally, I don't want to know what is considered "alternative punishment." Lydia is stuck with me, and I feel sorry for her. She deserves better.

"Can my partner and I come look at his room? There might be some clues there."

"Yes, that would be fine."

"Do you have a picture of David we can send out on the wire?"

"Yes," she says, moving the book from her lap to the desk. It is a photo album. She flips it open to the first page. "Lydia and David" is spelled out in colorful bubble letters and surrounded with stickers. Underneath, it reads, "Psalm 68:5."

"What's that?" I ask.

"It's kind of our motto. 'Father to the Fatherless—"

She keeps talking, but I don't hear anything else.

IV

After Lydia leaves, I sit at my desk mulling over what just happened. Until she spouted that phrase, I had viewed the past two days' weirdness as random events. I had been certain it was all a glitch in the Life Mod system. But this is beyond glitch. This is intentional. Even I can't convince myself it is a coincidence that her motto is the same as the statement uttered to me the day before by a disembodied voice when I was standing next to her. Using a cognitive recall trick, I think back to the first time I heard the voice. I was flipping through Marv's charity cases. What were the names? Mentally, I go back to Buttoned-down Marv's bland bedroom. I feel the mattress settle as I sit down. I hear the smooth roll of the drawer along its gliders. I feel the thick cardstock of the folders. I see the names. "Boles, Carter, Gondeck, Haw... Hawthorne!" Lydia and David Hawthorne. Could it be them? Has Marv worked for them? *This is too weird. It has to be some phase of Life Modification* They *didn't mention in the book.*

But that seems unlikely. Too many of the book's rules have been broken for this to be part of the programming. Besides, felons who've been through the system talk, and I've never heard a story remotely like this. Usually, they talk about what they did with the wives and girlfriends or how strange life in the twenty-first century is compared to the twenty-fourth. What can possibly be normal about clothing boutiques for dogs?

I decide to bury my head in the cases and not think about it. As I always say, the best way to deal with something that makes you uncomfortable is *not* to. *Nose to the grindstone, Smullian my boy. All you have to do is survive the day.*

My mantra, however, is not working. In the back of my mind, I wonder what will happen if tomorrow is no better. As a distraction, I force myself to focus on being Benigno. I straighten my posture and ease back into proud, married, Latino detective mode. Then I walk purposefully (I am sure that Benigno always walks like his destination is of vital importance, even if it is just a trip to the copier) over to my partner's desk. "Coward," I say.

Cheshire Charlie gives me a rueful grin. "Bad story?"

"Yeah, it's bad. I'll fill you in on the way to her place. First, we've got to send his picture out to our agencies as well as Georgia and Tennessee as a possible runaway."

Charlie grabs the photo and studies the earnest face looking out from the surface. "Good-looking boy."

"Yep, like his sister. Blond, blue eyes. He'll be road candy if we don't find him. Name's David Hawthorne."

Charlie shakes his head. "If these kids had any idea what goes on out there, they'd never leave home. Fuller from Economic called about the Clausen case while you were with what's-her-name."

"Lydia."

"Lydia," he says, letting the word roll off his tongue. "Fuller says all the accounts are empty, not just payroll. He interviewed the company's owner. Turns out he signed over all signatory authority to Clausen and took his hands out of the day-to-day operations six months ago. Get this, it was Clausen's idea. The owner was griping about his blood pressure, and Clausen suggested a sabbatical for the man's health. Clausen had worked for him for years and was always trustworthy, so the owner thought nothing of it."

"Robert's had no oversight for six months? No one's that trustworthy." *Maybe the owner should have taken a* **mental** *health sabbatical.*

"Nope," Charlie says with a touch of glee. "Man, when will people ever learn?"

"If they learned, I'd be out of a job," I say, amused at my own double entendre. Financial Planning Lesson Four—maintain dual signatures on all accounts, or don't sign over your finances to someone who insists on being called Robert.

Whether Robert planned it initially or not, he'd worked a long con. In a long con, people have time to get to know you, people have time to miss their assets, and you have a substantial chance of getting caught. He probably thinks he's gotten away clean, but the police are on his tail. It is only a matter of time. All the greats—Cassie Chadwick, Arthur Orton, Cartosh N7q, just to name a few—died in prison or went nuts.

Since neither option works for me, I prefer short cons. They don't yield as big a payout, but people usually never even know they've been hit. *Heck, sometimes they thank you for taking their money.*

"I checked with security at Jax International and Amtrak. They've received and distributed Clausen's photo. Miller's on the bus station. He's got a new case, too." Charlie adopts a serious look. "Some bag lady reported that her cat, Elvis, is stealing her hair pins. She wants him arrested. I told Miller we had a litter pan in holding."

I give the Benigno-appropriate light laugh and return to business. "I'll get this picture on the wire. Then we can head over to David's and Lydia's apartment."

"Hey, did you notice how she filled out the back of those jeans?"

"No, I did not."

Of course, I did. Here she is in her darkest hour, and I was checking out her well-formed glutes. What can I say? I'm a dog.

"Just 'cause you're married doesn't mean you can't appreciate the scenery."

I love the way Chuckles thinks, but I'm not me. I'm Benigno.

"She's a child," I say, with proper indignation. "Maybe if you stopped watching the scenery, you'd hold onto a woman for longer than three months."

"Ouch," Charlie says, clutching his chest. "Not all of us are lucky enough to meet a woman as great as Marisol."

"She's one-in-a-million."

"I just want you to know, Benny, if anything happens to you in the line of duty, I'll make it my personal mission to make sure all of her *needs* are met."

"You could try, but she's too much woman for you. And don't call me Benny."

Charlie laughs good-naturedly as we walk to the car. I fill him in on the case on the way to Lydia's apartment. He thinks the same thing I do—David is on his way to Nashville. "Little twerp," he mutters as we knock on the door. "She gives up everything for him, and this is how he repays her."

Lydia opens it and leads us inside. I make perfunctory introductions as we assess the apartment. It is small, two bedrooms with a dining-slash-living room. Charlie leans over to me and whispers, "I know some foster kids that would give their eyeteeth to be in a home like this. Little Twerp."

Chuckles hit the nail on the head. This is a *home*. Lydia has gone out of her way to make a welcoming environment. One might dub the furniture style early-garage-sale, but each piece sports coordinated colorful pillows and throws. The table displays matching placemats and napkins. Sunny curtains cover the windows and framed pictures of the family hang on the walls.

"You've done a real nice job with the place," Charlie says.

"Thanks," Lydia answers.

"This is a lot to maintain on a waitress's salary."

"David gets social security. It's still tight though."

While they are talking, I feel the room closing in on me. My heart bangs against my ribs. It becomes harder and harder to breathe. I need to get out; I'm suffocating standing there. "I left something in the car," I say, practically bolting for the fresh air. I don't even wait for an answer. Upon arriving at the car, I open the door and lean inside. I need to support my story in case one of them looks out of the window. My breath comes in quick gasps, and I exert every ounce of self-control to suppress hyperventilation.

"I hate this day. I hate this day. I hate this day," I grunt through clenched teeth. "How can everything go to flarp in such a short time?" The truth is, when my mom died, I'd have given *my* eyeteeth to live in a home like that. But I didn't have a grandma, or sister, or, even, a third cousin twice removed to take care of me. I had to do what I had to do. Here is David being handed everything on a platter—a family, a roof over his head, meals on a regular basis—and he is flushing it away.

Before I can stop it, my memory slams back to the colony hospital where my mom took her last breath. Galwa wasn't blessed with the high-tech medicine found on more populated planets. The cancer ate her from the inside out. At twelve, I was slight for my age and the cavernous hallway that led to her room swallowed me. The light burned her eyes, so the two of us sat in the dark. Days before, she'd said, "I love you, Smully," but uttered nothing since. That didn't keep me from hoping she'd speak again. Then her hand slipped from mine, and I knew I was alone.

I force my mind back to the present and try to control the shivers that course through my body despite the Florida heat. I've been gone from the apartment too long. I don't want Charlie coming to look for me, but I can't get hold of myself.

My cell rings forth with "Smooth" by Carlos Santana. I check the caller ID. It's Marisol. I think about letting it go to voicemail, but with her about to pop out the baby any second, it might be important. *Maybe I'll be forced to round out this twisted day by playing birth coach.*

"Hello," I say in the steadiest tone I can manage.

"Querido," she says. My body calms in some kind of Pavlovian response to her lilting, accented voice. "I know you're working," she continues in Spanish, "but I just wanted to tell you I love you."

It is ridiculous, cheesy, and completely sappy. Yet, it works. I know she isn't saying it to me, but in that moment, those words are what I need to hear. I exhale slowly and feel all the tension leave. *Maybe wives aren't totally useless.*

"Te amo tambien," I say before hanging up. I close the car door and walk back to the apartment.

"What took you so long?" Charlie asks.

"Marisol called."

"Can you two go longer than an hour without talking to each other?"

"Nope, it's called love."

Charlie is holding a coffee can and lid in his hand. It is covered with bright paper and reads, "Rock the Universe!!!" Chuckles stares into it with a puzzled expression.

"Where's Lydia?" I ask.

"She's getting us the numbers of people in Nashville," he pauses, then yells down the hallway, "When's the last time you put money in here?"

"Night before last," her voice echoes back.

"How much had you saved?"

"With those tips, it was $387.12."

Charlie looks back into the can, snorts, and tips it in my direction. There's nothing inside but the reflection of the ceiling lights on the bottom.

"When we find that twerp, I'm going to wring his scrawny little neck," Charlie says without a hint of humor.

Not if I do it first.

V

ydia takes the can from Charlie and thrusts her hand inside as if the emptiness is an illusion. After several seconds of digging, she gives up, sets the can on the table, and looks at the two of us. I wait for the geyser of tears to begin again. I wait for the crumpled girl to re-emerge. It doesn't happen. The feisty woman is still in firm control.

"This isn't what it looks like," she says, planting her fists on her hips.

"What does it look like?" I ask.

"You're going to play that card? I have enough problems without you guys treating me like I'm stupid."

"We're not—" Charlie starts.

She interrupts, putting up an impatient hand. "I know it looks like David took our money. I know it looks like he went home. But he didn't. If he wanted to go to Nashville, he would have told me. David wouldn't have taken off without a word. Something else is going on; I don't know what, but it's something. It's your job to figure it out."

Sure, take it out on us instead of the little twerp who skipped with all your loot.

"Ms. Hawthorne," I say in a placating-the-victim tone, "We understand your concerns and, I can assure you, we are never less than thorough. However, it is *our job* to investigate all possibilities, even the uncomfortable ones."

Lydia isn't put down that easily. "I don't want you focusing on Nashville and forgetting to look in Jacksonville."

I am gripped by two conflicting desires. One, to grab her and throttle her for being so *bletted* naïve. The other, well, I'll just say a spunky woman who knows her own mind excites me in a special way. I can't indulge either impulse because I am stuck in the body of Captain Discipline.

So, I clear my throat to show Benigno's self-control and continue evenly. "Ms. Hawthorne, you have my promise that we will exhaust every avenue at our disposal and follow every lead that crosses our path." I am not going to back down, though. She needs to understand we aren't going to avoid the runaway scenario just because she doesn't like it. I add, "Regardless of where it takes us." Frankly, I don't care where it takes *us* because I am out of here at the end of the day.

She takes a deep breath and exhales. It is clear she isn't happy but has decided not to argue any further. "I don't mean to give you a hard time. I know you're doing your job. But I know my brother. This isn't like him. My other brother Jesse was the hardheaded, rebellious one. If it were Jesse instead of David, I'd be thinking just like you.

"David's," she pauses, fumbling for the right word. "David's sensitive. Well, more sensitive than most teenage boys. He's into art and music and drama. He'd leave a note or something. He wouldn't just take off," she finishes, turning and walking down the hall. "His room's in here," she says, striding through a doorway.

Chuckles slides up next to me and asks, "How many times have we heard that?" Then he puts on an affected feminine voice. "I've known my husband fifteen years. He's a good man. He wouldn't cheat." Then he shrugs and drops to his normal tone. "Yet we still find him in a seedy hotel wrapped around a nineteen-year-old."

I chuckle in response and clap Charlie on the shoulder. "Isn't that the truth? Do we ever come across someone who lives up to what their loved ones say about them?"

"Nope, everyone's up to something," he says, then whips out his Cheshire smile. "Except you and me, of course."

"Well, me at least," I add.

"You said it, Benny Boy."

"Benigno."

David's room is like any other teen's, which means it looks like New Orleans after Katrina hit. Clothes cover every inch of carpet and most of the desk. Only a fitted sheet shields the bed, the other covers lay in a heap on the floor. Band posters and hand-drawn renditions of album covers paper the walls.

"David's?" I ask as I point to a sketch of a man in a trench coat with angel's wings.

"Yeah, he's good, isn't he?" She appraises the drawing as if seeing it for the first time. "You'd think it'd get old, his art, but I'm always amazed."

The only thing that keeps me from gagging outright at the sappiness is the fact that she's right. The twerp is that good. I notice a CD cover with the same picture lying on the stereo and his copy was Xerox quality.

After I scan the rest, my eyes settle on his bedside table. There are two framed photos. One is of the entire family. Mr. Hawthorne and Jesse had darker hair and eyes than the other three, but they were all unmistakably related. The other picture is of Lydia and David in the apartment's living room. I recognize the yellow curtains behind them. Lydia's hair hangs loosely around her heart-shaped face and she has a wide smile, all pink lips and white teeth. This is what she looks like when her world isn't falling apart around her. *Man, I wish I wasn't pretending to be married.* David's smile isn't as wide as hers, but he looks happy. He doesn't look the part of the sullen, miserable teen. A kid capable of swiping his sister's jack and running off without leaving a note wouldn't have shots like this in his room. Lydia must have put them there.

"Would you be able to tell if anything was missing?" Charlie asks. He opens his eyes comically wide and gazes around the room.

Lydia giggles. "Actually, yeah. I'd need a little time for an inventory. His duffle is right there, though." She gestures toward a rumpled nylon bag near the closet door. "Wouldn't he have taken that with him?"

She'd stated in the intake interview that David's backpack was gone. I decide not to point out that a backpack would be much better on the road than a duffle. I know this from experience. It's always best to have your hands free if you can manage it.

"That's everything for now," I say. "We'll keep you updated if we learn anything new."

She follows us to the front door. "Are you going to talk to Mrs. Granger? What about his school?"

Chuckles turns on the quarterback charm. "Yes, ma'am. She's next on the list. 4B, right? We'll be out to the school as soon as we can."

"Yes, she's in 4B." Lydia continues to hesitate in the doorway, her hand resting on the knob. She turns and looks into the living room and then back at us. "Should I come with you?"

She doesn't want to be alone in there. I want to walk off with Charlie but can't. The thought of her alone, worried, and scared in this apartment holds me like a gravitational force. *Not your problem, Smullian my boy.*

True, I argue within myself, but Benigno would care. It is my job to emulate my host as much as possible. So for the sake of appearances, I decide to give her something to do. It's for the character, and certainly not because I am worried she'll go nuts sitting in the empty apartment. And if you believe me, I have some land for you on Tricon 4. "You know what would really help us?" I ask.

"What?" she responds, her blue eyes hopeful.

"Two things, actually. Could you call some of those people in Nashville and see if they've heard from David? And also, it would be great if you could do that inventory of his room."

She looks relieved, almost eager.

I hate that I care.

"Yeah, I can do that," she says. "I'll get right on it. Should I call you when I'm done?"

Please don't, you're complicating my day. "Yes, that would help us a lot."

Charlie's phone rings as she is shutting her door. He answers and after a few "yeps," he hangs up. "That was Fuller. They picked up Clausen at Jax International."

"Good, one more thing off the to-do list. I guess I need to call the secretary—Melinda was her name. She's not going to be happy." *Oh great, another crying woman. Haven't I suffered enough?*

I feel like someone is driving a spike into my forehead just over my right eye. I glance at my watch—it is barely one o'clock. This is, hands down, the longest day of my life. Until now, that honor has been held by the day I tested for Life Modification. "Every candidate for Life Modification will undergo a battery of physical, neurological, and mental examinations to determine aptitude for Life Modification therapy and the processes within," per the book. In other words, *They* want to be sure of two things: number one, that you won't go psycho and leave a trail of bodies moldering somewhere in the twentieth or twenty-first century (like the brainhitcher in Jack the Ripper did in the 1800s); number two, that you actually have the brains to carry out all those meaningless tasks while pretending to be someone else. It's not surprising that most felons don't qualify.

"You okay?" Charlie asks me.

I know I'm acting weird. Time to revisit the I'm-not feeling-myself scenario.

"Still a little queasy," I say, patting my stomach.

"We'll grab lunch after Granger," he says as he walks toward apartment 4B. Then he stops and looks back at me. "If I catch this from you, you're in deep trouble. I do not throw up."

I laugh. "Maybe you'll luck out and only get the other part."

Chuckles screws up his face as if he'd smelled a banadox. Think dead skunk kind of stench. "Serious beat-down if I get sick, I'm tellin' you."

I laugh again. "Don't be a baby. I think it's something I ate, so you can relax."

"Yeah, well, it better be."

"Why don't you go ahead with Granger while I make that call?"

Charlie nods and walks away. I flip through my notepad looking for Melinda-the-Secretary's number. My objective is simple—pass her off to Fuller in Economic Crime as quickly as possible. I identify myself and immediately start the blow off. "I'm calling to inform you that Robert was detained at Jacksonville International Airport. If you have any further questions, you can contact Detective Fuller in Economic Crime." *Clean, neat, quick.*

"Why was he at the airport? What's Economic Crime?"

Not so quick. Stick to the company line. "Fuller will be able to answer all of your questions."

"I don't understand. He was leaving?" I can hear the tremor in her voice. The tears are coming.

Third time's the charm. "Detective Fuller should have *all* the answers. You can contact him through the main switchboard. Just ask for Economic Crime, and they'll connect you."

"He was leaving me." I can hear her sobbing on the other end of the line. "Did he take the payroll, too?"

Maybe if I answer one question, she'll be satisfied enough to call Fuller. "Well, the accounts are empty. He is a person of interest. However, that's not my department. It's Fuller's area. He's the one who can give you more information." *Take the hint, lady.*

The sobs now elevate into outright blubbering. Melinda forces words between intakes of breath. "I trusted him. We all did. I feel so betrayed."

Clearly, I need a new tactic. She said the magic word. The word used by con artists, customer service representatives, and salesmen alike to overcome someone's objections and bend those objections to a desired outcome. Yes, I intentionally listed those three professions together. The way I see it; I got pinched for doing the same thing customer service reps and salesmen do legally. It isn't fair. I do, however, take solace in the fact that grifters hold a certain roguish allure while those other guys are universally despised. I mean *universally*. There are some planets where tax collecting is considered a more noble profession than sales. But I digress.

The magic word is *feel*. By using the renowned "feel, felt, found" method, I would end this phone call.

"I understand how you feel. Anyone would feel that way in your position," I begin.

"How could I be so stupid?" she asks.

"You're not alone. Other victims of crime have felt the same way."

"What do I do?"

"Others have found that a little information goes a long way toward easing those feelings. When you contact Fuller, he can give you information about the Federal Office for Victims of Crime."

"I think I'll do that," she says. The blubbering slows down to a few sniffles. "Thank you for being so understanding."

"No problem." *No problemo, indeed. One more monkey off my back.* My spirits improve, and I join Cheshire Charlie. Either he or Mrs. Granger has left the door open, so I give it a quick tap before entering. The two of them are seated in the living room, surrounded by cats. Charlie is trying to hold a professional expression while one particularly round feline kneads his thigh.

Mrs. Granger appears to have the same affliction as all pet owners, isn't-my-animal-the-cutest-in-the-worlditis. She strokes the cat closest to her and says to Charlie, "I named him Romeo because he's a little lover boy. Look how attached he is to you."

"I see that," Charlie's mouth says while his eyes are yelling, "Rescue me!"

"Hello, Mrs. Granger, I'm Detective Diaz."

"Hello," she says. "I was just telling your partner here what a good boy David is. He never complains about anything. He even cleans my litter pans when my back is ailing."

Of course, he doesn't complain; you're paying him.

"I couldn't imagine that sweet boy running off," she continues.

I glance at Charlie who is rolling his eyes and trying desperately to dislodge the very plump Romeo. "Has David ever mentioned Nashville to you?" I ask.

"Oh, all the time. To hear him describe it, you'd think it was heaven itself. He hasn't talked about it quite so much lately. Has he, Sir Puffington?" she directs to the orange tabby curled up beside her.

Sir Puffington? She'd be perfect for a pedigreed pet scam. You know, if I conned the elderly, which I don't. I have rules.

"What has he talked about lately?"

"School, this trip he and Lydia are planning. Waste of money if you ask me. I grew up in the Depression. We wouldn't have thrown away our hard-earned wages on some frivolous concert. Those two deserve some fun, but a trip to Orlando? Isn't that right, Sir Puffington?"

"You said you heard him leave yesterday."

"As I told your partner—look at how attached Romeo is to him—I heard David slam the door at 6:45 A.M. That's when he leaves to catch the bus."

"Is there anything you can think of that could help us?"

"No, I hope you find him soon. Poor Lydia, she must be eaten up with worry."

With one sentence, my light mood is gone. I picture Lydia in that apartment sifting through the twerp's things and crying. She's turned me into a sap in half a day. No more lying to myself. For whatever reason, it bothers me that she is upset. I really am going to wring that little twerp's neck. He's ruining my life.

"You know, she'd probably like some company," I say. Even though Mrs. Granger was clearly off her rocker, I know Lydia would like someone to be with her.

"I wonder if she's had lunch. That's the first thing to go—appetite. People get upset, and they quit eating. I lost eight pounds when Mr. Granger passed." Normally, eight pounds isn't that much to lose, but Mrs. Granger resembles a dry spaghetti noodle. She must have looked like one of those kids in the Food for the Nations commercials.

We excuse ourselves and make our way to the car. Charlie is all grins. "I considered pulling my weapon on that cat. I'm sure there's a section about animal attacks in Code of Conduct."

I glance over at him and notice he is covered in cat hair. He either isn't aware or doesn't care. I look at my own pants and discover the same thing. I don't care, but Benigno the metrosexual would. Chances are he has a lint roller in the car. *Glove box or side door pocket?* I decide on the side door pocket. Benny would have his ticket book and other work-related stuff in the glove box.

When we arrive at the car, I open the door and reach into the storage compartment. My target rests right at hand. It is good to know I'm not totally off my game. I put my left foot on the seat and go to work removing Romeo and Sir Puffington's leftovers.

"You called me a baby, and you're out here in the parking lot lint-rolling your pants?" Charlie asks.

"An earmark of a good detective is his neat, professional appearance. You could use it, too." I point to his Dockers with the roller.

Charlie looks down, gives his pants a couple of whacks, and shrugs. "Good enough," he says and climbs into the car. "Let's go to lunch."

I finish up, returning the trousers to their pristine condition. "Sounds good," I say as I throw the roller into its place. I could eat a three-course meal, but I must maintain my cover. "Somewhere with soup."

VI

We eat at one of those trendy places that serves food and provides Wi-Fi. The tables are crowded with college students hunkered over textbooks and middle-aged businessmen answering emails on their laptops. Noises of clanking utensils and people chattering surround us. The aromas of coffee, hot bread, and soup fill the air. I love it; the hustle and bustle has me buzzing.

I neatly tear apart my bread and dip it into the soup, taking a bite. Chuckles stares at me over his burger. I notice he hasn't started eating. *Great. Benny's not a dipper.*

"You're not gonna pray?" he asks, disbelief in his voice, merriment in his eyes. "Doesn't that mean you have to go to church like twice on Sunday or something?"

Bad tradecraft, Smullian. You saw the devotion book. I pat my belly. "This virus, man." I bow my head and repeat a prayer on the chip. "Bless us, O Lord, and these thy gifts, which we are about to receive, through thy bounty through Christ our Lord we pray. Amen."

"*Thy? Bounty?* You're breaking out the holy words today. You must be in real trouble," he laughs. Chuckles recounts a recent football game while mauling his dripping cheeseburger. His hand can barely contain the inch-tall patty, onion bun, and fixin's. The tomato and lettuce keep slipping out of the thick sandwich. Ketchup and mustard ooze from of the sides. My soup loses flavor while I watch him enjoy such a masterpiece. *First the Krispy Kreme, now this. I don't care who I am tomorrow. I'm eating a steak.*

During lunch Charlie keeps conversation to everyday things: football, zombie movies, actresses he doesn't think are as hot as everyone else does. I figure he and Pretty Boy have a no-talking-about-the-case-at-lunch policy, and I appreciate the sentiment. It doesn't work though; my mind is on fire. Questions flick through my brain like sparks from a lighter. I've known plenty of stunning gems in my day. Why is Lydia getting under my skin? It was the tears, had to be.

What is David's problem? He has the best gig an orphan could ask for: loving sister, nice house, his own stereo. All the rules of self-preservation state he should keep his skinny rear at home. Why run off? Unless things aren't so peachy, but I can't imagine Lydia as an evil sister with a sweet façade.

Who is this *Father to the Fatherless* and why was he bugging me? What does that even mean anyway? I wonder if I should read Psalm 68:5 when I get the chance, but then discard the notion as quickly as it surfaces. No need putting in more work than necessary, especially over a system glitch. Nothing pulls my strings. I know that sounds funny, considering They have literal control over my body, but my thoughts are my own. I choose to cooperate with

Life Modification because it is in my best interests. I have every intention of returning to my nefarious ways when I get out of the clink. Behaving is the quickest way to get my life back.

"Seriously, those huge eyes and puffy lips set in that skinny face. Yuck. I guess I'd understand if someone had a Mistress of the Dark fetish, but she does nothing for me," Charlie says.

"Who?" I mutter, feigning interest.

"Who? Angelina. Are you even listening?"

"Sorry, man."

"Dude, you're not all here. Maybe you should go home. Let me finish up the interviews."

It is tempting. For a second, I welcome the notion of lying in bed, staring at the TV, and letting Marisol take care of me. Having her around has really opened my eyes to the benefits of matrimony: the Sprite, the sweet phone call, the worrying about me, er, Benigno. I picture her hovering over me, boring into me with those bottomless dark eyes, and realizing something isn't right with her husband. Yeah, I can't handle an entire day with the wife. It'd be way too stressful. I'll have to keep taking my chances with Chuckles.

"Go home and trust you with all the paperwork? I don't think so," I say.

"I said *interviews*. I was going to leave that for you," he answers with his Cheshire grin.

"Did you do any of your homework in school?"

"I was captain of the football team."

Nailed it. Man, I'm good. I mentally pat myself on the back for excellent tradecraft while he continues.

"As long as we were winning, there was someone around to free up my time so I could concentrate on the team. If we were losing, there was someone willing to ease my burdens and comfort me."

"Were these *someones* female?"

"You know me too well, Benny Boy."

"Benigno."

On the way out, Charlie brings the case up. I guess the no-talking thing only applies when at the table. "We agree he ran off?"

I nod.

"How's he getting to Nashville? I don't think he'd spend the majority of his precious $387.12 on plane tickets. Bus seems the most logical." *We should send Miller. He already spent the morning there on the Clausen case. That would be hilarious.*

A mischievous look crosses Charlie's face. "I hope Miller's made it back to the office. It'll make it more fun when we send him back." He lets loose a rousing guffaw. "I wonder if his bag-lady girlfriend is still there."

Great minds think alike. "You should take it easy on the rookie," I lecture in my best Benigno tone.

"Give me a break, Benny. Our pay stinks, the hours stink, the only perk we have is picking on the rookies."

"Remind me again why you do this job."

Chuckles' trademark smile vanishes. His blue eyes settle on mine. "Carrie, my sister's best friend. You know that."

"It was a rhetorical question."

"Look Benigno, I know you think I don't take this job seriously, but I do. I joke around to let off steam. I could have gone to narco or robbery, but I chose this. It's not a stepping-stone for me. I know how a person vanishing affects a family, the entire community. I'm peeved at this David kid for acting like a schmuck and worrying his sister, but I hope we find him before some predator does. So, don't get all high and mighty with me." The absence of his smile changes the set of his face. His jaw and cheekbones look roughhewn out of granite. His eyes look like two raw sapphires mined from deep in the dark earth. He is fuming. I gotta defuse this quick.

This version of Chuckles is a formidable guy. I could say that years of self-preservation have taught me to immediately neutralize a tense situation, and that would be true. But the baser fact was that I don't want Charlie mad at me. Being the cause of that anger is uncomfortable. That's the problem with letting people into your life; they knock you off balance, make you *feel* things like discomfort. To be able to affect a person's emotions is power, my friend. Nobody has power over Smullian O'Toole, other than Smullian O'Toole himself. But I digress.

I need to get rid of stone-face Charlie and return Cheshire Charlie. If we were women, I'd have to go into some spiel about how I was sorry and didn't mean to get him upset. He'd go into some monologue about how I didn't appreciate him. Blah, Blah, Blah. Good thing we aren't women. This can be solved with one sentence.

"You're sexy when you're angry."

Charlie doesn't burst out laughing, but he does offer an appreciative sniff. Then he rolls his eyes and produces a slight smile. "I'm telling Marisol you were hitting on me again."

"I know what'll make you feel better. David had to get to the bus station somehow, right? Maybe he took JTA. Call Miller and tell him after he's done at Greyhound, he can go to the JTA terminal."

His trademark smile and chuckle are back. He slaps me on the shoulder. "It's a pity offer, but I'll take it." He grabs up his cell phone and makes the call.

"Hey Miller," Charlie says. "Do you have plenty of Meow Mix? We need you to head back to the depot with a picture of that David Hawthorne kid. Thanks." There is a pause while Chuckles tries very hard not to laugh. "Oh, I almost forgot, when you're done there, head over to JTA and do the same thing." He taps off his phone and shoves it in his pocket.

"I love that kid," he says to me. "We're going to get a lot of mileage out of him."

"Time for the high school?" I ask.

"Yep, the high school. It's still shorts weather," he adds with a grin.

"They're children."

"I wouldn't date one—what kind of a guy do you think I am? I'm sayin' if they didn't want me looking, they wouldn't dress that way."

I couldn't agree more.

VII

I approach the school with some degree of fascination. Education is handled vastly differently in the twenty-fourth century. On Earth and its colonies, there are three different types of schools. Poorer colonies like Galwa are driven by industry. The school's sessions are determined by the timing of the harvest or the hours at the factory. Child labor laws still exist, but on those planets the age of adulthood is thirteen. Where was our great universal government when that decision was made?

Anyway, those kids only have an elementary or, at best, middle school foundation. Populations are small and infant mortality is pretty high, so the ones lucky enough to be school- aged attend the equivalent of one-room schoolhouses and, unfortunately, the teachers know barely more than the children.

The middle-income planets have large auditoriums where the students are taught by a holographic teacher. The governments cut way down on cost by having one teacher per discipline educating the entire population. Richer, more advanced spheres, like Earth, distribute learning cubes (a sleeker, smarter distant relation of the

PC) to each child. They are then tutored within the comfort of their own home by hologram.

Budding grifters named Smullian were lucky enough to avoid all forms of formal schooling. Life is a far better teacher.

On Venox, a non-human planet, adolescence is considered a form of insanity and all youth are kept in stasis until they've "returned to right thinking." Those kiddies are educated via an implanted data stream while they sleep. They reach adulthood and wake-up—smart, refreshed, and ready to serve society.

The metal detector and the uniformed cop in the school's lobby make me think maybe the Venoxians are onto something. Charlie nods at the boy-in-blue with professional courtesy, and we make our way to the front office. We explain what we need to the harried woman behind the counter, and she produces a list of teachers for us. Then she says something that stops me cold.

"Why don't you wait until school is dismissed? It's only an hour from now," she says as if we are children in need of discipline. "We prefer not to interrupt classes."

Does she think we're taking a survey here? I am not sure what irritates me more: her complete coldness toward David's plight or her lack of respect for our authority. The second emotion surprised me. I mean, I wrote the book on lack of respect for authority, and yet here I am, fuming because she thinks my job is trivial in comparison to her need to keep things on track. The worst part is I actually thought "my job," not "Benigno's job." I open my mouth to tell her what I think of *her* job, but Chuckles beats me to the punch.

"Ma'am, when you call the police, do you expect a timely response?"

"Excuse me?" she says.

Granite guy returns, and, I have to admit, I am happy to see him this time. "If a burglar breaks into your home, you call the police. Right?" he asks as if *she* were the child in need of discipline. "And when you call them, do you expect a timely response?" he repeats, the muscle in his jaw twitching.

"Of course," she says.

"Doesn't David Hawthorne deserve that same consideration?"

Her eyes dart to the side and she mutters, "Umm…"

"What about the other people that might need mine or Detective Diaz's assistance during that hour we're twiddling our thumbs here in the lobby waiting for school to get out? Don't they deserve the consideration of a timely response, or is that something only you deserve?"

Get her, Granite Guy.

She stammers for a moment, then grabs another sheet of paper and hands it to us. "Here's a map of the facility."

"Thanks," Charlie says with a smile that doesn't quite meet his eyes.

We study the map and make our way to the first classroom. The teacher, a woman, embodies casual, professional chic. For sure, she didn't buy her slacks and sleeveless sweater at the mall. That, combined with the silver clip grasping her hair, indicates wealth. *Hubby brings home the bacon.* She is shocked when we tell her David is missing. Her next response, however, confirms what Chuckles and I have been thinking. "Did he run away?" she asks.

"Why do you ask?" I respond.

"It's clear he isn't happy. He's, you know, withdrawn—draws all the time, doesn't talk with anyone. He does his work though, not setting the world on fire, but far from failing."

"Can you think of anyone he might hang out with?"

"No; as I said, he doesn't talk with anyone."

I thank her and we move on. The next two teachers have similar stories. Educator number four is the English teacher. He is a pudgy, middle-aged man without any deep concern for fashion. His mildly wrinkled cotton button-up appears like he'd pulled it from the dryer and hung it up without ironing. His hair has grown out of its cut and hangs limply around his ears. *Newly divorced and letting himself go? What a sap. Glad he's not my host.*

His story is different from the rest. "I had David last year. He's grown leaps and bounds since then. We journal every day in class, and his entries denote more hope than when he first got here. He wrote some pretty dark stuff in the beginning. I think he turned a corner over the summer."

"Other teachers have described him as withdrawn," I say.

"He's an introvert alright, but compared to last year…" He lets the last part hang as if it were explanation enough.

"What kinds of things does he write about?"

"Last year it was all about his family. Boy, there was some serious guilt in those pages. I tried to get him to talk to the counselor, but he wouldn't. This year, there's family, but more about the sister than before. They're planning a trip." A sly smile stretches across his lips. "There's been a couple about love."

Charlie snags that one. "He have a girlfriend?"

"I don't know if it's reached that level, but he's been talking to Madison. She's been writing about love, too."

"Madison what?" Charlie asks.

"Madison Fairburn."

"Does he write about Nashville much?" I ask.

"Last year, that was second only to family. He's only mentioned it once this year. He misses the leaves changing color. Have you seen any of his drawings?" We both nod. "He writes just as well. The setting he described made me want to walk through those woods."

"Do you think he'd try to go there?" I ask.

The teacher fills his cheeks with air and blows it out. He runs his left hand through his hair. When he does, I notice a faint tan line and indentation on his ring finger. Recent removal of a wedding ring. I was right.

"Last year, I'd have said an unequivocal yes. This year, it's possible, but I don't know how likely. He does seem to be adapting."

We thank him for his time and return to the office. When we ask about Madison Fairburn, the lady behind the counter is quick to point out we couldn't question her without a teacher present. Chuckles gives her a measured look. "I'm sure you know that," the fussbudget adds quickly. "She's in room 217. You only have a few minutes before the bell rings."

Room 217 isn't that far, and we make it there right before the teacher dismisses class. When we ask for Madison, the teacher calls over a girl who would never be described as pretty but stops short of the ugly line. She has flat (both in color and body) brown hair and pale skin. She wears a baggy t-shirt and jeans.

I am starting to wonder what David sees in her until she walks toward us. She moves with unexpected feminine grace—not as if she's trying out for *Star Model,* like the other girls I've seen in the school. When she approaches us, a gentle smile touches her face showing perfectly straight, white teeth. I notice the shirt advertises one of the bands David has memorialized on his wall. It's evident this quiet, unassuming girl would appeal to our runaway artist.

"Hi, Madison," I say. "I'm Detective Diaz."

"Hi," she answers, clutching her books to her chest.

"A teacher told us that you're friends with David Hawthorne."

"Yes," she says. A blush rises to her cheeks and then fades into a look of confusion. "Why are you asking about David?"

I consider beating around the bush but decide to be straightforward. "He's been missing for two days."

"I thought he was sick. I've called him, but he hasn't answered. I thought he was out of minutes and turned off his phone."

"Do you remember when you last spoke to David?"

"Sunday." The blush returns. This girl has it bad. Makes sense, David was a handsome boy, probably not the kind of guy that normally paid her attention. "We talked for like, two hours. His sister was at work."

"Did he mention if he had plans to go anywhere?"

"*Rock the Universe.* He was real excited. He's never been to Universal Studios."

Charlie chimes in. "He didn't mind going with his sister?"

"No, he thinks she's really cool." Her eyes shift. Cops and con men everywhere recognize little signs like this.

"But?" I ask.

"He feels bad."

"Bad about what?"

"Well, you know, she should be partying, not hanging out with a kid."

"Does he ever talk about what happened to his family?" Charlie asks.

"Yeah, it's terrible. I couldn't imagine. My parents get on my nerves, but I love 'em. You know."

"Anything else about his family?" Charlie prods.

"He and Jesse, his brother, had a big fight before the crash. David was all mad at him and that's why he didn't go to the soccer game. He feels real bad about that." She pauses, biting her lip. "He's okay, right? You'll find him?"

I think about Lydia; she asked me pretty much the same thing. *What is it with women extracting promises I can't keep? Tomorrow I'll be long gone. Then this will all be Benigno's problem, and he's much better equipped to deal with it.*

"We'll do our best," I say. "Can you tell us the places he likes to go?"

"He doesn't have a car, so he walks or rides the bus. He hangs out at the diner where his sister works. He goes to the library near his house. He really likes the park. Last week, he drew me this." She flips open her notebook and shows us a detailed drawing of a spider in its web. David drew water droplets on the silk that practically sparkled.

"Can I go?" she asks. "I'll miss my bus."

"Call the station if you hear from him, even if he asks you not to. It's important that we find him."

"What if I just want to know what's going on?"

"It's okay to call for updates. Ask for Detective Charlie Weidhoff," I answer.

Chuckles and I head to the car. "Thanks for pawning the girlfriend off on me, Benny."

"I owe you for sticking me with the intake interview, and it's Benigno."

"Touché, Benigno," Chuckles says, emphasizing each syllable of the name. "Maybe David's not as much of a twerp as I thought," Charlie muses.

"What do you mean?"

"He's got a lot of guilt. Maybe he thinks Lydia's better off without him."

"He'd be the type to fall for that misguided line of reasoning," I say. Lydia's face pops into my mind again. I wonder if she is okay. "Maybe I should call the sister and update her on all of this."

"Not a bad idea. She might have some info from Nashville," Charlie says. "It's strange, though."

"What?"

"A guy doesn't tell a girl that stuff unless he likes her or he's a player. And David ain't a lady killer."

I understand immediately, but I play dumb. "What's your point?"

"Take off when you've got a babe on the line? It's strange."

"I agree. I don't think he planned this. I think something triggered it."

"Maybe the double shift. He starts feeling guilty about sis having to work all those long hours. Thinks about how she's better off without him. He sees the money jar and BOOM, he's out the door."

"Works for me," I say. "Let's head back to the office. We need to follow up with the other agencies and send out some uniforms to the library and park with his picture."

I give Lydia a ring to check what she'd found out from David's Nashville buds.

"This is Detective Diaz. Did you get any information from David's friends?"

"I sent you an email with all their names and numbers." I scroll through Benny's inbox and click on the one from Lydia. It lists five names.

"I have it."

"I reached Tyler, John, and Richard." *That leaves Josiah and Chase. I'll check with them later.*

"They haven't heard from him in a couple of weeks," Lydia continues. "And when they did talk to him, he didn't mention coming to visit. He would have mentioned it to them. He would have told them if he was planning on going. But he didn't, which means something else has happened, right?"

Of course, they could be lying. Teens have been known to do that. I'm inclined to believe them though. If Charlie's and my theory is correct, David took off on the spur of the moment out of guilt. He wouldn't call ahead and make arrangements. What worries me is that if our theory is correct, he might never call anyone. If he really is stressed about being a burden, he might just want to stay off the radar entirely, which would make my job—I mean Benny Boy's job—much harder.

I should end the call here, but what can I say? I like her voice. Plus, it's clear she needs to talk, and I don't have the heart to cut her off.

"There are many angles to consider. How are you holding up?" I ask with my best Benigno concern.

"I'm okay, considering. Mrs. Granger came over earlier, and I'm keeping busy. Lots of praying. David's friend Madison is coming over in a bit. I'm fine."

"How are you, really?"

"How does David have a girlfriend, and I don't know about it? Yeah, he is a private person, but I'm his sister! Shouldn't I know something like that? Maybe I don't know him as well as I think I do. Maybe I work too much and don't have enough time for him. Is that why he's gone? He feels neglected. How can I give him more time? I'm barely holding us together as it is. If he ran away, I failed him. I didn't take good enough care of him. Maybe it was a mistake bringing him down here. I should have moved to Nashville. But where would we have lived? I couldn't keep up the house payments and property taxes. Plus, I'm still hoping to finish my degree. If I moved to another state, it would be harder and more expensive to get back into UNF. Nashville universities would have different course requirements; I'd have to retake classes. But if that's what he needs, that's what I'll do."

Man, I never want to be a woman. It's a wonder their skulls don't melt from the heat generated by that much thinking. I like having my mental compartments where everything has a place, there's a place for everything and nary the twain shall meet.

"That's a lot to be worried about. Breathe. I suggest you take one thing at a time. No need to plan a move or change colleges just yet. As far as Madison, that relationship wasn't a relationship yet. They'd barely passed the crush stage. Knowing your private brother, he was probably waiting until it was official to tell you about it."

"You're right. He wouldn't want to tell me about a crush and then have to tell me she didn't like him back. He would wait until he was sure. I feel like I'm in the dark. No information to light my way."

"I get it. The uncertainty can be scary."

"You have no idea. I'm stumbling around trying to find something to hold onto."

I wish she could hold onto me. I wish she could rely on me, but I'm not that guy, except I'm being that guy right now. My Benny mask has slipped, and it's me, Smullian, asking the questions, doing the reassuring, and really listening, not just paying attention. I'm a grifter. I lend quite an ear. My job and my life depend on what I glean out of a conversation. When I listen, it's for gain—gain of information, gain of fortune. I listen to determine if someone is worth my time and friendship, and so far in my life I've found no one is. Everyone is up to something. Everyone is a liar, a cheat, and a thief just like me. Except maybe Lydia…or Benigno…or Marvin. But I digress.

I'm just letting her talk. I have no agenda, no goal. I am truly listening to her uncertainty, pain, and fear. Is this all I can do for her? What if David isn't found? Will this be just another chapter in her short, tragic life? My muscles and gut tighten as the conversation rolls. What is this—compassion, frustration, worry? I have to face the fact that my Benigno mask has fallen, and I, Smullian, am feeling these emotions for another person. *When the deed is done, cut and run. Far. Or else you'll be trapped.*

I clear my throat loudly. The universal move that indicates a conversation has gone on way too long. I cap off the effect with, "Well, I have to get to some other case work, Ms. Hawthorne."

I choose my words precisely. They imply that she's nothing but a case number among other case numbers to Benny Boy.

"Um, okay," she answers. I can hear hurt and confusion in her reply. What had seemed like a therapeutic release to her was clearly an imposition to Detective Diaz. I could feel her embarrassment at having gushed forth in a socially inappropriate manner. "I'll wait for your call. Goodbye."

She says the last so quietly, I almost don't hear it. The feisty woman that had called me to task earlier in the day is gone again, and the wreck from this morning is back. I feel a bit guilty for that, but it's for her own good. The sooner in life she learns that you can't rely on others, the better.

VIII

I do busy work until I am sure that Marisol has gone to bed. I am fairly certain she will retire early. From what I hear, women that late in pregnancy are practically narcoleptic. Charlie had left a couple of hours earlier with a quip about how he'd never work late if he had a woman as pretty as Marisol at home. I snorted something about responsibility, duty, and paperwork in response. I hate to admit I was a little sad to watch him go. I like Charlie and will miss his banter wherever I find myself tomorrow.

At Casa Diaz, I find a plate of food and some flan in the fridge complete with a sweet note about how proud Marisol was of Benny Boy's dedication to his job. As I nuke the leftovers, I think about the note. This day, I learned that police work is a high pressure and often tedious task that is defined more by paperwork than car chases and taking down perps. It must be nice for Benigno to come home to some appreciation.

After eating all of my meal and most of the flan, I make my way to bed. I've heard married men say that they can't sleep without their wives beside them, and I've mocked them. Everyone knows men don't like snuggling. Anyone who does like it is whipped. So why am I enjoying the simple pleasure of having Marisol curled up beside me? I know she's isn't my wife; I don't even think about her that way. My thoughts in that area are disturbingly fixed on Lydia. Yet, all the stress of the day and the casework fade away by the mere warmth radiating from Marisol's frame. I feel content, as if all is right with the world, even though all is clearly *not* right with the world.

I reconsider my previous philosophy on marriage. The right wife, at least in Pretty Boy's case, can build you up instead of bringing you down. Marriage isn't for me; I need to stay footloose and fancy free, but I might think twice before judging a guy who chooses it. *Look at me being all evolved.*

I decidedly do not like where my thoughts are heading. It is clear to me that Jacksonville, Florida, is a cursed city. If this glitch doesn't get fixed quick, I might actually become the respectable citizen *They* want me to be. That is unacceptable. The only solution is to will myself to sleep and hope that tomorrow I am not only someone else, but somewhere else.

I walk back in the cop shop. Night settles ominously on the place. Shadows linger in strange places when no people bring life to the building. Someone announces over the loudspeaker, "The Father to the Fatherless on line one." Then every phone on every desk starts to ring. I run out of the room and into another. Only it isn't another room, it is the same one. I stand in the doorway and watch Lydia. Her diner uniform resembles armor. The powder-blue color makes her eyes shine. Standing near Benny's desk, she is surrounded by a faint glow. She is luminous, literally.

I walk over and stop next to her. She doesn't know I'm there. "Something has happened to him and it's your job to find out what," she commands the person sitting in the chair. Then she leans over and jabs him in the chest. "Your job."

I turn to look at the person, expecting a Puerto Rican detective, but find instead a man in his mid-twenties. His appearance, chin-length shaggy brown hair, and his posture, slumped to the side with arms crossed on his chest, exhibit disregard for everything. I hear the clack of his shoe on the Formica as he leans forward, plopping his elbows on the desk. He shifts his hazel green eyes up at her and smirks. "Not my job, baby."

She jabs him again, "It's your job whether you like it or not."

Every phone rings again, crescendoing louder and louder. I run from that room into the same room, but the furniture and Lydia have vanished. The hazel-eyed man sits alone in the corner, his knees drawn to his chest. The room morphs into a hospital hallway, and the man becomes a boy. He hides behind his hair and cries. Phones shriek in the background, their dissonant peals echoing off the walls.

I wake with a start, sitting upright in bed. My breath comes in ragged gasps. The covers are tangled around my legs. I am trapped and pulling at sheets makes it worse. Marisol stirs beside me and I feel her soft hand on my arm.

"Está todo bien?"

No, everything is definitely not alright. "I'm fine," I answer in Spanish.

She rubs my arm and then falls back to sleep. I lie down beside her, hoping for her magic touch to put me out. But I can't shake the dream. I expect the bedroom to disappear at any moment, and I'll be back in the cop shop with the phones ringing, staring at myself. I haven't seen my own face in 778 days and didn't recognize it in the dream. Its sudden appearance is disturbing, to say the least.

When my heart refuses to return to a normal beat, I ease out of bed so as not to rouse Marisol and go to the kitchen. Even from the stairs, I can hear the flan calling my name. I don't think about the dream while I polish off the remainder. I am sure this is the kind of thing the shrinks at Life Mod live for—a dream rife with possible symbolism, returning me to the trauma of my youth. If I were a patient instead of a detainee, they'd probably want to schedule all kinds of special sessions. Well, they aren't here, and I'm not going to afford this episode any more merit than it deserves.

Granted, certain aspects of the day remind me of my youth, and the past couple of days have been bizarre, but that is all the portent I will give to the dream. I am stressed. Who wouldn't be? I'm being tricked. One of Life Mod's goals is to make me "empathize with my victims." They almost accomplished that today. I certainly came close to that emotion with Lydia and David, but that was as close as they are going to get me. I will scrape those two off me, just like I am scraping the crumbs off my plate into the sink. (Benigno would never leave a dirty dish on the table.) I finish with the plate and set my heart. *They*, or whoever, will not win this.

While some of the aspects of David's case lead to more questions, the fact that he's run off did not change. The bigger fact, that this is Pretty Boy's and Chuckles' problem, doesn't change either. Who are *They* kidding? I'll be someone new tomorrow, what can I possibly do anyway?

After I excuse myself of any responsibility, I return to bed ready for some Zs. They don't come. A question pops into my mind. Why didn't David leave a note? All accounts paint him as a sensitive, thoughtful kid. Even if our he-feels-guilty-for-ruining-Lydia's-life theory is correct, it seems like he'd leave her a note explaining his actions. He'd want to release her. So why didn't he leave one?

I try to ponder other things for most of the night, but the question keeps returning. Somewhere around six, I feel an intense burning in my abdomen. Then it feels like someone is forcing hooks through my skin and tearing it open. Imaginary Vikings grab hold of my lungs and rip them through my ribs. I welcome the pain. It means this day of uncomfortable truths and more uncomfortable questions is finally over. Blackness creeps over me as I say good-bye to Benigno.

PART THREE

AGGRESSIVE BARGAINING

I am over the throne, slinging hash when I wake up. Same thing happened on the Japanese whaler: the host's body stays on autopilot until the brain-hitcher takes complete control. Good thing too, because I couldn't have made it to the john as sick as I am. My host's stomach totally empties, but that doesn't stop his body from pumping. After numerous dry heaves, I slump down between the toilet and the wall. My cheek rests on the smooth floor. I keep my eyes closed, concentrating on the darkness and the coolness seeping into my face from the linoleum. The world still feels like a downward spiral, and I am a hapless passenger.

Biotransposing while awake is beyond painful; it's torture. In twenty-first century America, the bleeding hearts would have Life Mod deemed unconstitutional by the eighth amendment.

However, in my time, The Powers-that-Be formed a subcommittee to look into allegations that Life Mod was "cruel and unusual punishment." For two years the PanEarth Tribunal on the Proper and Ethical Treatment of Human and Alien Offenders bickered over the intricacies of case law, both past and present. Finally, they ruled, "Life Modification does not violate any being's rights because the detainee is in control over his/hers/its state of wakefulness and therefore chooses his/her/its own level of discomfort." The document was over four hundred pages long, but the opening sentence summed it up pretty well. I didn't choose to have insomnia last night, but I doubt anyone at the tribunal is going to rewrite that masterpiece over little old me.

My host's cell phone rings in the next room, and I wait impatiently for it to switch to voicemail. After that crazy dream, it reminds me of B-rated horror film's score. I try to stay calm while my host's body adjusts to my unwelcome presence, but the bewitched phone keeps going. Most stop after four rings, maybe six, but this one echoes on ridiculously. *What kind of psycho sets their voicemail protocol like that?* As it rings, my mind flashes back to the cop shop and the lost boy sitting in the corner.

Spinning world or not, I need to shut the infernal thing up. I can't handle standing just yet, so I crawl from the bathroom into the bedroom toward the insistent sound. Bumping into the bed, I send my brain on another spiral and have to wait while things settle. Meanwhile, the blasted thing keeps shouting at me. *When I find it, I'm going to smash it into bits.*

Based on the direction of the trilling noise, it has to be near the bed—maybe the bedside table. The room slows to a manageable level, and I hoist myself onto the mattress. I risk moving my head and look around for the boisterous culprit. This guy chose a headboard bookcase instead of a bedside table. My enemy balances near the ledge of its cubby, poised to fall onto a pillow. I watch as the vibrations from the ringing walk it across the shelf.

Finally, my world normalizes, so I'm free to snatch it up. There isn't a caller; it's an alarm. This fact would have dawned on me, if my head wasn't spinning faster than Cornifu. Of course, the touch screen won't read my fingertip, so the thing keeps mocking me while I'm pressing the disable button over and over. It won't shut up, so I chuck it at the wall. It's bad tradecraft, but I don't care. Blessed silence fills the room. I try to relish the calm, but my eyes are already noticing things.

One glance around the room tells me this guy is a new divorcee. It isn't decorated at all. Blank, white walls stare at me. The windows have the blinds they came with—no curtains. He bought the prefab headboard from someplace like Target or Ikea. No bedspread, just a fleece blanket that could be bought at any box store.

Why divorcee? Bachelors equip their pads one of two ways. "Late-frat-boy" style—dirty clothes piled on the floor, neon beer signs on the wall, personal reading material on the bedside table. "I'm-sensitive-and-tasteful" style—professionally coordinated (either by a designer or the best friend's wife) color scheme, modern art on the wall, classics on the bookshelf. Widowers, on the other hand, have a more lived-in look because they want to keep everything as the wife left it, and there are pictures of the family everywhere. Neutrality dominates this guy's place. It screams, "My wife got everything and all I have left are my clothes." So, newly divorced.

Speaking of clothes, my guy sleeps in a white t-shirt and briefs. Okay, Average Joe. I run my hand over a slightly curved belly, confirming that thought. If American, my boy definitely enjoys chili-cheese fries and a beer on occasion.

I lift my left hand, noticing an indentation and faint tan line. There was a ring not long ago. I grin and literally pat myself on the back. *You are the best, Smullian my boy...* My thoughts trail off and my stomach knots again as I remember David's newly-divorced, pudgy English teacher from the day before. *No, it can't be.* I plunge my hands into his hair to confirm my suspicions. Average Joe's hair feels about six weeks past due for a haircut.

"No," I shout, jumping out of bed. I pace the length of the room and back again. "This isn't fair. I was a *cop*, blast it. Isn't that worth something? Haven't I earned a simple job like garbage man or plumber?" I look at the ceiling because it seems the most logical place to direct my attention and shout, "Hey, are you listening? I don't deserve this."

I know *They* or whoever can't hear me, and I don't care. I had to say it out loud. Lydia's line from the dream comes back to me. "It's your job whether you like it or not."

"Well, I don't like it, and I'm not going to play your twisted game!" I clench my fists and kick at a blanket on the floor. It blossoms up and floats back down with a whisper. I don't even get the satisfaction of a loud thunk. I'm not even sure what I'm madder about: finding myself once again in Jacksonville, Florida, or having to teach high school.

The seeming randomness of the last two days now has meaning. Everything leads back to David. It isn't a coincidence, and it sure as drak isn't a system glitch. Of all the people I'd talked to yesterday:

cops, waiters, gas station attendants, and so on, I wake up inside the one man who had more than a professional concern for that little twerp. What makes the schmuck so important?

"I am the Father to the Fatherless," echoes around me. *I'm hearing voices again. Fabulous.*

"I don't care who you are. No one tells me what to do," I bark into the empty room. Silence responds. "Is that statement supposed to be some kind of answer to my question? Is David important because he's an orphan? Yeah well, I was an orphan and there were no disembodied voices hijacking felons to protect me when I was young. Where was this almighty Father when I needed one? Nowhere. I had to scratch and claw my way to survival. David isn't better than me; why should he get a break?"

Frustration rears its head when the stupid phone wouldn't quit ringing. Nah, I'm way past that emotion. I am livid. "This is going too far. It's coercion. No—blackmail. What kind of person uses another's tragedy for their own ends? I've conned a lot of people, but I've never done that. You hear me? I have rules."

Without thinking, I slam my fist into the bathroom door. White-hot pain burns up my arm and chases away all my thoughts and feelings. Blank space dwells between my ears, only throbbing exists. Clear thought returns. Okay, I am drastically overreacting, but, in my defense, wooziness from that drakked biotransposition still lingers, and that dream frayed my nerve endings. I have a right to be angry. Someone is jerking me around, but it doesn't constitute violence. Thinking about it makes me even madder because normally I'm a very laid-back guy, and someone knows all my buttons. "I'll show you. I'll stay home."

When the pain abates, I gingerly close my hand into a loose fist. Crackles of pain gallop up my arm, but I can move my fingers. *Not broken, good.* I glance down and see raw knuckles and drizzles of blood dripping over Average Joe's mitt. Plausible excuses for the wound spring into my head. When you've been on the grift since before you could walk, some things, like damage control, happen by reflex.

I am enraged and, possibly, bowling with only eight pins, but I need to act in my own best interests. Staying home to spite this person or persons will only get me more time in Life Mod. "Hey. I won't be staying home today, but not because you want me to be this teacher. I have only 221 days left of my 1000-day nut, and I am not going to let some lunatic on an ego trip trick me into making it longer."

Besides, there is the con. There is always the con. Teaching won't be an issue. I talk a mile a minute, and I know a lot about a lot of things. I learned early the secret to hooking a mark was finding a common point of interest. So, I read anything I can get my hands on and consume a lot of media. Things haven't changed just because I am in the clink. I may be in a new century, but I am still on the grift. Without breaking any laws, I con people every day. The money is just a side-benefit; the performance gives me the real thrill. I will be Average Joe Teacher, busted hand or not, and no one will notice. And I will do it without lifting a finger for David Hawthorne.

However, I'd rather be lion taming in some Ukrainian circus than herding adolescents all day. *Are whips against school policy?* This host confirms that The Powers-That-Be at Life Mod aren't involved. Not only are there laws in both the present and the future prohibiting felons from teaching, the book has a rule about it. "The candidate's exposure to minors will be limited in order to preserve society's ability to direct the path of its future citizens." In other words, they want to keep us hoodlums from corrupting impressionable young minds. I've never been in a host that has prolonged contact with the under-eighteen set. I look forward to the challenge.

I tuck my anger into a quiet corner of my brain and get back to work. First, I must take care of the hand. Losing control like that is bad form, and I am still unhappy with myself for doing it. But no need to dwell on such things. A quick search of Average Joe's bathroom doesn't turn up any first aid supplies, not that I expected any. Women think to stock up on band-aids and triple antibiotic ointment; guys don't think of those items until they're needed. Then they usually improvise with duct tape and a kitchen towel. I rinse off the wounds, which rank as little more than scratches, and wrap a washcloth around my knuckles. I'll buy some gauze and tape on the way to work. It seems like pharmacies are Jacksonville's main industry. I'll find one within thirty seconds of the apartment.

The lack of wound care items emphasizes the bathroom's emptiness. Most of Average Joe's toiletries dwell in a Dopp kit. Only his toothbrush and toothpaste are stored in the medicine cabinet. It would make sense if he'd just moved in, but the tan line on his ring finger has mostly faded. I'd say he removed his ring somewhere between six weeks and two months ago—plenty of time to get settled into his new pad. He could have stayed with a buddy for part of the time, but I have a hunch that isn't the case.

I opt out of showering and head to the closet. I know what clothes I'll find. I saw Teacher Boy yesterday. As expected, the closet holds jeans and casual slacks. He possesses an assortment of colored tees and cotton shirts. He even owns sweater vests. Can't get more teachery than a sweater vest. I'm dying to wear one, but Florida only has two seasons: February and summer. It is late September; so, I opt out on the sweater vest.

After dressing, I retrieve the cell phone from the floor where I'd flung it. A nod to the manufacturers—it exhibits no noticeable damage. The phone doesn't have the graphic of a half-eaten piece of fruit, either. Teacher guy cares enough about his technology to eschew the mainstream. *I bet I'll find role-playing games on his computer.*

The top of his dresser sports nothing but spare change. I snatch it up and put it in my pocket. From his waistline, I can tell Teacher Boy likes to hit the vending machines at school. I don't have his first name, but I do know his last name from the interview yesterday. Mr. Burns. I am more interested in confirming my hunch about him being here for a while than tracking down this guy's moniker. The name doesn't present a challenge. I'll learn it as soon as I find a wallet.

I have some extra time because I know the school's location. I've become more familiar with Jacksonville than I'd ever dreamed possible over the last couple of days. There won't be time wasted hunting up maps and worrying about getting lost this morning.

I scan the bedroom again. Except for the shelf the phone was on, the bookcase headboard is crammed with books. They aren't in any particular order; they look like he's just thrown them up there willy-nilly. The bedroom is unpacked, but certainly not "settled into." If he'd moved in recently, empty boxes would be cluttering up the place—maybe not in the bedroom, but somewhere in the pad. My senses, honed by experience, tell me I won't find any.

I step out into the living room. One chair, one TV, and one bookcase, also crammed with books. A gaming console is at the ready on the floor. I power it up and eject the disk. As I thought, it is a role-playing game. *Sometimes it hurts to be this good.*

The dining room isn't a dining room. He's set up a cheap desk and converted the space to an office. There are stacks of folders, presumably papers waiting to be graded, along the wall and a cork board with a large calendar. It holds teachery info like assignment due dates and holidays. I turn on the computer and step into the kitchen while I wait for it to boot up.

Most of the cabinets are empty. One holds paper plates and plastic utensils. His fridge has beer, Coke, and creamer. The freezer is stuffed with pizzas and frozen dinners. Next to the coffee maker is a single cooking pot. My assumptions have more than enough circumstantial evidence. Average Joe has been here awhile. The place is arranged to meet his needs. It is unpacked, in a manner of speaking, and there isn't an empty box in sight. There is only one explanation—deep down Mr. Burns was holding out for reconciliation with Mrs. Burns. He hasn't settled in because he still hopes to move back home. I guess no one has told him that when a woman serves you with divorce papers, she's not playing hard to get.

The only contradiction to this is the ring, or lack thereof. He probably took it off so he wouldn't look needy. I am sure it is tucked into a safe corner of one of his dresser drawers. I am also willing to bet that he didn't lose everything in the divorce. He gave it all to her. Amendment to Financial Planning Lesson One—Don't make decisions based on emotion, or don't hand all your money over to the skirt who's ditching you. *What a sap.*

Thinking of Mrs. Burns brings Lydia to mind. I wonder how she faired the night. Did my rebuff on the phone make everything worse? I remember how the crying had distorted her beautiful face yesterday and head for the phone. I need to fix it. I need to tell her everything will be okay. The receiver is in my hand before I override the compulsion to call and see how she is doing. Maybe Mr. Burns isn't such a sap. Some dames are dangerous.

There is nothing in the kitchen that could be described as breakfast. Salisbury steak washed down with creamer is not going to work for me. I step back into the "office" to check the computer and hunt for Burnsey's wallet. As predicted, there are short-cuts to notable RPGs on the computer desktop. There was also a folder titled "lesson plans." Perfect. I click it open and scroll through the file names until I find one with today's date. I print it out and give it quick read through. They are studying *The Merchant of Venice.*

"But love is blind, and lovers cannot see the pretty follies that themselves commit," I quote out loud and add, "That one's for you, Burnsey." I've been memorizing the bard since I was a teen. Even in the twenty-fourth century, a well-placed quote from Shakespeare could trick a mark into thinking you're respectable and trustworthy. As if the ill-intentioned can't enjoy the classics. Dickens will get you far, too, in most circles. Of course, *The Merchant* also holds Financial Planning Lesson Number Five— "All that glisters is not gold," or if it sounds too good to be true, it probably is.

I not only read Shakespeare for the job, but also because I love it. The plays, especially the comedies, are ripe with cons and deceptions. Heck, a con artist saves the day in *The Merchant,* or that's how I interpret it. Teaching is going to be a breeze.

Burnsey's billfold is next to the keyboard. I snap it up and flip it open. The driver's license picture is obscured by its leather frame, so I wrestle the card out to get a better look. Average Joe Teacher's real name is Keith. Keith Burns—a perfectly normal American name. How average. His picture resembles a mug shot, but whose doesn't? As I am shoving it back into place, I notice a photograph peeking out from the slot. I tug it out.

Bingo! I had concrete proof about Burnsey's romantic delusions. The shot is of a much younger and thinner Keith. He is all smiles and dressed in a tux. His arm is draped around a radiant brunette dressed in a white gown. What divorced guy keeps his wedding photo hidden behind his driver's license? Only a schmuck hoping to get back with his wife. It is kind of sweet, in a pathetic way. I feel sorry for him. His marriage obviously mattered to him. I wonder what went wrong. People always assume it's the guy who messes things up, but I've known plenty of heartless women. I have a feeling that was the case here.

I glance down and realize the wallet has been sitting on an open Bible. My eyes slide over the glossy page and I find, to my dismay, Psalm 68 is listed at the top. Did he plant this here? He? Where did that come from? It feels right, though. I've acquired sufficient evidence to eliminate The Powers-That-Be at Life Mod as being in charge of the chaos of the last few days. Today's situation does more than break the rules. It destroys them. Not to mention, the push to Christianity. Separation of church state rises to a whole, new oppressive level in my time. It can't be a glitch either. The code monkeys who observe the endless algorithms driving the system would have caught this by now. I'm thinking one guy because he keeps saying, "*I* am the Father to the Fatherless." It's some smart, tech savvy, exceedingly annoying guy who fancies himself the protector of all orphans. Textbook delusional narcissism.

There are only two ways he could have planted this Bible here. One, he walked in and did it, but that would mean he was in this century. If he were in this time, he wouldn't have access to the tech necessary to override Life Mod. I don't even know if Life Mod has that kind of tech. He could have used time travel, but that is highly unreliable and dangerous. There is no way he could pinpoint a date, time, and place this exact. Besides, what could possibly be so important about David to compel such a risk?

The other logical possibility is that he brain-hitched Burnsey and set up the book. However, brain-hitching is a tightly regulated industry (remember Jack the Ripper was a hitcher) and has sharp penalties for unauthorized travel.

Perhaps there's not a logical explanation, and I'm okay with that. In my time, we have tech that so far surpasses twenty-first century imagination it would seem like magic to my hosts. We have mapped more of the universe than people in this century could ever conceive of existing. What has all that knowledge taught us? That we don't know as much as we think we do. Truly, anything is possible.

Let's forget "how" for a moment. Why? Is he out to get me? Is this some revenge-fueled plot? I'm the best, which means I know not to pull long cons. Big jobs breed retribution, not my small fry stuff. Besides, I doubt there's some cosmic Keyser Soze bending time to settle a score with little ol' me. It's more logical he's concerned with David. But what could possibly be so important about the twerp to justify such risks.

I may not understand how this father guy is working, but I'm sure there is some angle. I just don't see it yet. One thing is for sure. I'm not playing *his* game. I slam the Bible shut, quoting Antonio from *Merchant,* "The devil can cite scripture for his purpose."

Nose to the grindstone, Smullian my boy. I grab up the briefcase sitting by the front door and head out. Keith's keys tell me he has a Nissan. I sigh, remembering Marvin's Ferrari. My fingers ache for the smooth leather interior. I wonder if Marv's gotten it back from the cops yet. Poor guy. I bet he was in agony yesterday knowing that his baby was in the hands of strangers. An odd sensation grips my insides, kind of like someone is tightening a belt. Is that what guilt feels like?

Can't be. I have nothing to feel guilty about. When someone buys a car like that, they should expect it'll get stolen. Just because Marvin never drove his Ferrari, and it happened to get nabbed when I took it out, doesn't make it my fault.

Or does it?

I shake my head and force my thoughts back to Keith's car. The chances of him having a Z, or even better a GT-R, are slim. Even if he could afford one on a teacher's salary, he gave the heartbreaker everything of substance. No, all I could expect was some mid-size four-door with more than a few thousand miles on it. What a day I am going to have: lame car, lame job, and trapped in the same lame city. I do my best Eeyore imitation, slumping my shoulders, and saying "Oh, well."

There is only one Nissan in the vicinity of Keith's building—an Altima. I start to walk to the driver's side when I see that the neighboring car is parked over the line. In fact, it is so ridiculously close there was no way I can open my door wide enough to shimmy inside. The driver had either been drunk or a woman.

The only option is to enter the passenger side and climb over to the driver's seat. This day is just getting better and better. The anger from earlier starts to rise again, and I put a tight lid on it. I've already proven to myself how unproductive that can be. I open the trunk and toss in the briefcase. Then I walk around to the passenger door. Once in the seat, I crouch and stretch my host's leg toward the driver's side. It is clear Burnsey hasn't kept up with his yoga. The muscles in his thigh object to the action, but I work through the pain. That done, I shift until I am sitting on the middle console. I slide Keith's ample posterior into the driver's seat, but my right leg's still stuck on the passenger side. I try to move it toward me, but it is wedged on the dash between the radio and the glove box. I have to grab the leg behind the knee and heft it over, banging it on the steering wheel in the process. "Drak it to Neth," I grunt through clenched teeth as a wave of pain explodes from the spot. Finally in the correct place, I sit for a moment, catch my breath, and temper my frustration. "Burnsey," I say, "you have got to lose some weight."

Physical fitness is as important to grifting as knowledge. I'm not talking about being some muscle-bound gym rat whose idea of a tense run is when he uses the mountain terrain setting on his treadmill. I'm talking about being able to run a mile as if your life depended on it, because frankly, in the con game, sometimes it does.

There was this one time when I was on Theta Outpost, a customs-slash-fueling station without much else except half a dozen bars. The only people there are sailors, shipping execs, and beings of questionable character who are drawn to that kind of environment. Usually the shipping execs are smart enough to stick to their vessels, but not that night. There was this pair of young pasty-faced fools standing at the bar as if they belonged. Their suits probably cost more than the building, and they were flashing cash like everybody carried around that much loot. I think they actually believed the two females draped on their arms were interested in them. One of the ladies was a Jenshurian, which are famous for their "special" skills. I wouldn't know. Call me a speciesist, but I prefer my women with two arms and no tail.

I have rules. I don't grift anyone doesn't deserve it or who can't afford it. These guys fit both criteria. I couldn't resist. They were begging for it. Besides, someone was going to get their money, better it be me than someone who'd do more than steal. These suckers would be light on cash, but at least they'd have all their organs when I was done with them. Normally, I don't rush into a grift without some reconnaissance, but, as I said, I couldn't resist. It was supposed to be a walk.

I pulled a wooden top out of my pocket and invited them to a friendly game of "put and take." The game is simple. You spin the top and if it lands on the "p," you put in money. When it lands on the "t," you take out money. Of course, it's fixed—spin the top clockwise and it lands on "p;" spin counterclockwise and it lands on the "t." The game is a centuries old con, but it still works in the twenty-fourth. People in my time, especially educated people, are so attuned to electronics that they are fascinated by low-tech items. They find things like tops and dice quaint, even primitive, and thus innocent. The thought of tampering never enters the mark's mind.

I played these guys like a violin. First, I let them win to build their confidence. Then I slowly bilked them out of almost every, well, the closest translation is dollar. It was sweet. However, it turned out they weren't as stupid as I had assessed. They didn't figure out the con, but they'd had the forethought to hire bodyguards. If I'd done some reconnaissance, I'd have known that fact. The rent-a-muscle watched the guys lose with some amusement until it dawned on the hires that their pay was disappearing with each twirl.

Next thing I know, I'm being sucker punched. Meathead number one's fist had landed squarely on my jaw. I was dazed for a second, but still had the presence of mind to grab the cash. As meathead number two was connecting with my stomach, I dropped to the floor and rolled under a table. I made a mad crawl to the front door while the meatheads were throwing tables left and right, trying to get their hands on me. All the while the pasty-faced shipping execs were hollering things like "Hey," and "What's going on?" What fools, all that ruckus and they still didn't have a clue.

Once at the door, I found my feet and blazed out of there. The meatheads followed and almost caught me in the first few yards, but that was all it took for me to gain the lead. I ran until my lungs burned and my legs yelled for relief. Then I climbed up a transmitting tower and counted my haul. In the morning, I bought myself passage on the same boat the shipping execs called home. What's better than a free ride? One bought with ill-gotten gain. But I digress.

I doubt I'll have need for that kind of tactic at the high school. I turn the ignition and sputter off toward my new job. I mentally replay the conversation with Burnsey and me, er, Benigno the day before. Based on that and Keith's place, I know he is a concerned teacher who attempts to engage his students. The guy reads and remembers what they write daily. Of course, that means I am going to have to appear interested in those self-centered, self-indulgent brats. When I was a teen, I didn't have the privilege of agonizing over whether Jenny "liked" liked me or whether Mommy and Daddy were going to get me the latest gaming console. I was too busy fighting off pervs and worrying about where my next meal was coming from. You know, it's adolescents who would benefit from Life Mod. Let them spend a day as Smullian the teen and see how they "learn the value of an honest day's labor." The anger dances around my brain, but I manage to suppress it.

II

A t the school, I have déjà vu again, but less startling than at the cop shop. Being in the same environment throws me less than yesterday. Right away I notice two kids playing keep away with a third one's smart phone. The third is fruitlessly jumping up and down, reaching for the device. Panic radiates from his eyes as he says, "Please, I just bought that. It took me two months to save up." The other two just laugh.

Wish I had a taser. Burnsey wouldn't use a taser, even if he had one, but I am certain he would intervene. I stride over to the group and hold out my hand. "Give it to me."

"What?" One of the boys asks, feigning innocence. I hope law-breaking is not his intended career path because he won't make it far with that act. I choose not to speak, but instead level my gaze at the offenders and wait. After a tense moment, I raise my eyebrow.

"We were just playin' around," the boy says as he places the device in my hand.

"Mm-hmm," I respond, still staring. The two drop their eyes to the ground and shift their feet. "Get to class before I write you up." They belong in detention, but I am also certain that Burnsey is a second and third chances kind of guy.

"Yes sir, Mr. Burns," the boys answer in unison as they speed toward the building.

I hand the phone back to its owner. "Do you have somewhere safe to keep that?"

"Yes," he mumbles. "Thanks, Mr. Burns."

Keith would probably deflect the whole gratitude thing; I wave it away with my hand. "Remember, you're not supposed to have that out in class," I say in my most teachery voice—a little paternal concern mixed with rebuke.

"Ye...yes sir," he stammers, shoving the device deep into his backpack. I wait until he walks away to smile. Maybe some parts of the job aren't going to be that bad. I like bossing people around.

While teaching is mentioned in *The Exhaustive Lexicon of Twentieth and Twenty-First Century Labor Practices,* process and procedure vary from country to country. In the States, it varies from school district to school district. There's no way the *Lexicon's* researchers could gather all that data, much less place it on the chip in my brain. I only possess some vague information about educational theory. The front office seems like a good place to start.

The fussbudget from yesterday is behind the counter again. Papers are spread out before her, and her collating ability rivals most automated systems. She wields a stapler with skill and precision while smiling and nodding at every teacher that enters. She is the ruler of this world, which explains her behavior toward Benny Boy and Cheshire Charlie yesterday—anything that enters her realm has to be put firmly under thumb. I chuckle quietly as I remember Charlie's not-so-gentle rebuff to her. *"Ma'am, when you call the police, do you expect a timely response...or is that something only you deserve?"* Good times.

My mirth dwindles and disappears into the anger that had been simmering all morning. In this century, Charlie and I could have been buds—same sense of humor, same outlook on life. Instead, it had been a one-day show. Why tease me with the concept of friendship and snatch it away? I need to get on top of this situation before the Father ruins me for good. I am already experiencing uncomfortable emotions. What's next—remorse, love? Something must be done.

"Morning, Mr. Burns," Fussbudget says, interrupting my reverie. She doesn't even look up when I enter the room. Her evil, teacher-detecting radar functions on a wide bandwidth. "The field trip forms are in your mailbox."

I want to ignore her, just pull the forms out of the cubby and leave. The last thing I need to give her is affirmation. That is, after all, what fuels her power-hungry empire. You may say, "What power? She's only the secretary." That's a misnomer which has served women well for generations. A man *has* to be recognized; he *has* to have the flashy title. Women are content to be in the background, pulling the strings, resting in the knowledge that they're really in control. "Behind every good man, blah, blah blah." She may have a lowly position, but I'll bet the principal doesn't make any decisions without running them by her first.

Keith would be completely unaware of these undercurrents. He is probably grateful to have someone so organized and efficient in the office. I am Keith. I am forced to do what he would do, not what I would do. I give her a lopsided grin and say, "You're a lifesaver. I don't know what we'd do without you." I can see her power meter hit full tilt.

Her voice says, "You're too kind, Mr. Burns."

Her eyes say, "Don't you forget it."

I grab the stuff out of my box and glance around the room for a sign-in sheet or a punch clock. I don't see anything. Pretending to look through my papers, I wait for another teacher to enter. Only a couple of minutes pass before one does. It is one of the teachers Benny interviewed the day before. Warner? Waters? Watson. Her hair is in a bun this time, but she is dressed in the same type of chic, professional digs. The clothes are quality, which means someone in her life is comfortably employed.

"Morning, Keith," she says.

"Morning," I answer, watching her every move. She empties her box and drops a note in someone else's. Were I in the mood, I'd swipe it. There is something about the way it is folded that inspires questions about its content. All I can muster, though, is a fleeting curiosity.

"What happened to your hand?" she asks.

I'd forgotten about it. Pain relievers and a clean dressing from the pharmacy, which was less than a block from Burnsey's place, effectively pushed the matter from my mind. I actually look at my hand before answering the question. I roll my eyes and chuckle self-effacingly. "I was moving the TV, and it slipped. Rapped my knuckles good."

"Ouch," she says. "Sorry."

I shrug. "Things happen. Right?"

"Right. No serious damage."

"Nah, just scratched up a little."

"Oh. Field trip?" She points to the forms in my hand. *Just sign-in or whatever so I can do it and get out of here.*

"Yeah, I'm a glutton for punishment," I respond.

"Where are you going?" It feels like she is trying to think up things to talk about. Why doesn't she just get out and get on with her day, so I can get on with mine? I immediately run through all the field trip possibilities. They are studying *Merchant*—shipping, loan sharking, courts, the theater. While a visit with a loan shark could be quite educational, a stage production seems most likely. Jax is a port town, though. They could be doing something related to that. I am about to wing it with the theater bit when I am interrupted.

"Good morning, Mr. King," Fussbudget says. The man she speaks to is rugged, buff, and dressed in an athletic suit. Gym teacher. Has to be. Watson and he lock eyes briefly. Their intense gaze makes *me* want a cold shower.

"Keith. Mrs. Watson." He addresses both of us but keeps his eyes on her.

"Good morning, Mr. King," she adds, a light blush climbing up her neck. The forced civility, the formal address all say one thing—Mrs. Watson is getting a little personal training. I figure the suspect note is for him, but I don't bother watching to see if he goes to that box. Adultery never amuses me. The exchange does explain why Watson was hanging out in the office instead of leaving. I give up trying to discern the sign-in procedure and walk out. I know Fussbudget will stop me if I do something improperly. She doesn't.

I slip off toward my classroom. *This day can't end fast enough.* More by reflex than interest, I scan the halls and students as I go past. There are the requisite couples fused together, the loners plugged into musical devices or books or both, there are the clusters of kids huddled like jackals on the prowl, and the smaller groups that don't fit any category.

The girls are as expected—young and scantily clad. I'm not a perv. I am just "enjoying the scenery" as Charlie would say. By the time I reach my classroom, though, I am bored with the display. They all look the same. The same dyed-blonde hair, the same clothes. I picture them going en masse, like stampeding elephants, to whatever store is cool this week. I am attracted, of course. All that flesh and makeup are going to draw the eye, but when I look at their faces, really look, they aren't all pretty. Some are stunners, great bone structure, porcelain skin, but they just blend in with the rest. Whatever distinctive beauty they possess is lost amid the sea of similar faces.

I've never really thought about it, but in the twentieth-fourth century, everyone is different. Having traveled all over the known universe and been exposed to all kinds of females, I have come to appreciate the variety. The same is true in Life Mod. I'm in a new country every day, current circumstances excluded. I'm exposed to the dark, husky Polynesians and the pale Brits. This store clerk in Thailand had the darkest, lushest hair I've ever seen. But I digress.

The point is—someone has worked a massive con on the American teen. While I am mildly disgusted, I am also impressed. A con seamlessly executed on that kind of scale deserves admiration. Lydia's visage jumps unbidden into my head. She stands out. I allow myself a moment to mentally linger over her features before I force the image away. *I've got to get out of Jacksonville. This city is ruining me.*

No students occupy my classroom, which is good. On the way to school, I developed a plan, a nutty plan, but a plan, nonetheless. I close the door and sit at Burnsey's desk. Clearing my throat, I say, "Okay, how about a deal?"

I am talking out loud to no one, again. It seems like the only solution, logical or not. I know that The Powers-That-Be can't read my mind, but they do monitor day-to-day activities. I assume The-Annoying-Ego-Tripping-Interloper does the same thing. Hopefully, he can hear what I utter aloud. I wait a moment, giving him a chance to respond. I'm not sure what I expect, but nothing happens.

I go on. "For some reason, you want me to help with David. I'm not sure what you think a grifter, bouncing from body to body, can do, but I'm willing to cede that point. How about this? I'll help today. I'll do whatever is in my power as Keith Burns to aid in the David situation. But to be clear, I'm not going to violate the terms of Life Mod. I'm not risking a longer sentence for you, David Hawthorne, or anyone else."

I wait again. Nothing. "In exchange, I want to be returned to my proper programming tomorrow. No more Jacksonville, no more risky jobs. If you can swing it, I'd like to be pool cleaner at a Caribbean resort. I think that's only fair, considering what you've put me through." I look around the room as if addressing a table of CEO's. "Do we have a bargain?"

My last word was still hanging on the air when the classroom door opens. In walks Maddie Fairburn. I'll take that as a yes.

"Do you have a minute?" she asks.

Of course, I do. I'm a team player. "Sure. What's up?" I answer.

She settles herself into a desk in front of mine. I appreciate again the grace with which she moves. Plain, though she is, she exudes femininity. David, an artist, notices the beauty in a spider's web. After my realization in the hallway, it becomes even clearer what he sees in her. She is unique among a sea of clones.

"I hung out with Lydia, David's sister, last night."

"I bet that was good for her. I'm sure she's been going crazy with worry," I say without thinking. It sounds like a Keith thing, but really it is all me. I am relieved Lydia didn't spend another night alone and worried. What is going on with me? Since when am I concerned about a chick's feelings?

"Yeah, we're both worried. She says the cops think he ran away."

"That is the consensus."

Maddie looks away, fighting tears. Then she looks back at me. "My parents are kind of old school. They want to get to know a guy before they let me go out with him. Mom met him here at school and said he could come over. He was supposed to come over tomorrow and hang out for the first time. Why would he..."

I know what she needs—the assurance that David really liked her. It is simple math in her head. David running away equals him never truly caring about her. According to all unspoken social mores, he is too good-looking for her. She probably figured it was all a dream from the first time they talked. The last thing I want to do is crush this sweet girl. I'd lie, if it was necessary, to keep her intact.

Here I am again worrying about a chick's feelings.

Fortunately, I don't have to lie. I remember Charlie's assessment. *"You don't take off when you're about to land the babe."* Her story adds credence to what Chuckles and I decided yesterday.

"The police don't think David planned it. They think something big happened, like a trigger, which made him take off." I lean forward. "I don't think he'd run off without a really good reason. It's just not like the David I know."

She relaxes. "Exactly, he's not that kind of boy." She rustles through her things and pulls out a sheet of paper.

"Lydia and I made these last night. We're going to pass them out after school. My mom said I could." She hands the paper to me.

It is a flyer. David's handsome, sincere face stares out of the page. Above the picture it says, "Have you seen this boy?" Below it is the police station's main line.

A barrage of thoughts rushes my brain—this flyer lost amid all the other ones in grocery store windows, Lydia, those girls shouldn't be out alone, more time with Lydia, why bother if he ran off? I take a second to sort them all out.

The runaway scenario bothers me. I meant what I'd said a moment earlier. The more I learn, the less likely it seems he ran away. However, he took the Rock the Universe money. What other reason could there be to clean out his and his sister's stash? The deal stipulated I'd do all I could as Keith Burns. It isn't in *his* job description to solve the case but helping is. I puff up my cheeks and blow it out like Burnsey did yesterday.

"Why don't I go with y'all? Three hands are better than two." I decide not to mention I think they need a man along. Girls never respond well to that one.

Maddie smiles. "That would be great! I knew you'd be on our side. I'll call Lydia and tell her."

"No, I'll call her on my break. It should probably come from me." Once again, my mouth answers before my brain. What am

I doing? I need less time with that woman, lest she infect me completely, and yet, here I am manufacturing excuses to talk to her. What am I, twelve?

"Okay," Maddie says. "We're supposed to meet outside after school." She pauses on her way out the door. "Thanks, Mr. Burns."

I wave the gratitude away with my hand and pretend to go through my grade book.

The Interloper better live up to his part of the bargain.

As she leaves, other students trickle in. Some pull out books as they sit at their desks, others talk with the person next to them. I search through Burnsey's papers, looking for a seating chart. I don't find one. Of course not, Keith probably doesn't have one. He'd be the kind of teacher that memorized all the students' names the first day and was comfortable with a modicum of chaos in his class—a dream for students, a nightmare for conmen trying to fill his Super Teacher shoes. I look through all his desk drawers anyway, just to be thorough. Nada. There is a Bible tucked in the bottom one, which I close without a second glance. I said I'd help; I didn't say I'd read that stupid verse.

What's my strategy for identifying the kiddies? I could use nicknames like "Baboon Face" for the girl who needs lessons in makeup application and "Studly" for the boy with all the piercings. Nah, Burnsey would never mock his students. Poor sap, he probably thinks he's making a difference. The best option is not to use names at all. I could do a lot of pointing and saying, "What do you think? Yeah, you." But that won't cover roll call. I mull it over some more. Aha, I can have another student do it. Genius, Smullian my boy. You can handle whatever *he* throws at you.

The final bell rings and three students slip in after it finishes its chime. If *I* were the teacher, I'd embarrass them by pointing out that the big hand is the minute hand and the little hand is the hour hand. I'm not me; I'm Burnsey. Instead, I wag a finger at them, and they grin sheepishly. Boy, that put them in their place. Announcements begin. There is going to be a pep rally on Friday (ooh rah), starting Monday cars without valid parking permits would be fined (I'm sure Burnsey took care of that), and there's going to be pizza and French fries for lunch (no wonder there's an obesity problem in this country).

When that was over, I point at a girl who was chatting throughout the announcements. A social bug like that is likely to know all the students' names. "Can you check the roll for me while I take care of some paperwork?"

"Sure, Mr. Burns," she says as she bounces up to my desk. She glances down at my bandaged hand and asks the inevitable. "Did you hurt your hand?"

My own answer pops out of Keith's mouth. "No, this is the latest Paris fashion." Flarp, I lost control, again.

She stares at me blankly for a moment, then giggles. "You're funny, Mr. Burns. No really, how'd you hurt it?"

Oh yeah, he's a real comedian. "Home repair accident. Can you get to the roll call?"

"Sure," she answers and begins to place checkmarks next to names in the roll book as I pretend to look busy.

In my continued role as *team player*, I ask the class if anyone knows anything about David. On Monday none of these kids would have been able to pick him out of a crowd, but today they all know him. "Didn't he run away?" some ask.

"I heard he knocked over a convenience store and took off," one says. Surprisingly, others nod in agreement. Gotta love the rumor mill.

"No, he hasn't committed any crimes," I respond. "It's not certain he ran away either. That's why if you know anything about what he did Sunday or Monday, it would help. You can come to me or call the main police line and ask for Detective Diaz." Of course, no one knows anything.

Once that business is finished, I walk to the front of my desk and begin my teaching career with a simple phrase, "Take out your books." The rest of the period goes pretty well. I only resist saying, "Did you actually read *The Merchant of Venice?*" about seventy times. I put on a stellar performance myself, convincing an audience of thirty-four that I am Keith Burns.

After class, I wander out into the hall to find a water fountain. All of the teachers are standing beside their classroom doors. It was clearly a procedural thing, so I stand next to my door, as if that was what I'd intended to do all along. I assume the teachers do this to better monitor the juvenile delinquents. No one could start a fight or get pregnant under the glare of all these adults. Although, I'm sure these wily teens could figure out a way, if they really wanted to.

I see Mrs. Watson looking around and absent-mindedly twisting her wedding ring—the universal sign of a guilty conscience. She'd better feel guilty. Some poor schlub is working his tuckus off to provide her with that massive rock as well as the designer clothes on her back, and she is repaying him by boffing the gym teacher. It's not like being single is taboo in the twenty-first century. Why get married if you don't intend to keep those vows? It's the same in my time. My dad wasn't under any societal pressure to marry. So why did he? He could have had a lovely interlude with my mom and moved on. She and I would have been a lot happier if he had. That's why I stay footloose and fancy free, no promises to break. No shattered lives left behind.

The bell rings and another period begins. To save my sanity, I decide to give a different ridiculous explanation for my bandaged hand every period. Based on chatty Cathy's response to my joke in first period, I can rightly assume that Burnsey has a sense of humor. This period my wounds are the result of an attack by a Ninja assassin. I do the David spiel and get the same results. Aside from the convenience store heist, there are other equally ridiculous rumors. One includes him running off with an older lady. I set things straight and go on with class.

I find it difficult to maintain poise with these kids. They come up with the most ridiculous excuses to leave the room, interrupt me in the middle of comments, and ask the inane questions. *Any teacher that doesn't end up killing a kid should be nominated for sainthood.* The bell ringing fills me with joy; it announces third period, Burnsey's break time. The notion of a quiet Coke delights me, certainly not the thought of calling Lydia.

III

don't want to call from the office. Fussbudget has sonic hearing, I am certain. Control of information would be vital in her power-hungry empire. She would have to use blackmail occasionally to achieve her ends. All evil overlords do. Of course, she wouldn't call it that, and her victims wouldn't recognize it that way. Fussbudget would say she is helping. Her victims would think they were doing her a favor for all her *help*. Here's how it would play out.

(*Scene begins in a typical school front office.*
It is neat and orderly. Sitting at the desk is Secretary Ratched.
Teacher Gullible enters from left)
Ratched:
Good morning, Ms. Gullible.
Gullible:
Morning.
Ratched:
You look exhausted, dear. You must have been up all
night with worry over that brother of yours. Tsk. Tsk.

Gullible:

(*looks down*) He just can't make it outside of rehab.

(*looks back at Ratched*) No one knows.

Ratched:

Don't worry; your secret is safe with me. Why don't I get
you a cup of coffee and file those lesson plans for you?

Gullible:

Thank you. That's so thoughtful of you.

(*Same setting. Several days later. Nurse Ratched and Teacher Gullible
are in the office. Another teacher is in the back of the room.*)

Gullible:

It's an interesting idea, Ms. Ratched,
but it seems like a lot more paperwork.

Ratched:

It would make things much smoother in the office,
but I understand. (*just loud enough to be heard by the
other person*) How's that brother of yours doing?
You know, addiction hurts the whole family.

Gullible:

(*in a low voice*) He's fine. Thanks for asking. You know, if
that new system will help you, I'll talk to Principal Puppet.
It's the least I can do after all you've done for me.

End Scene

I don't want to put Keith in the position of receiving her *help*
but using Burnsey's cell phone to make the call could be a little
sticky. He is an above-board kind of guy, and probably doesn't use

his personal phone for school-related calls to the young, single guardians of his students. I decide to check the break room. It is possible the Duval County School Board treats the teachers like children and limits phone use to the office for "budgetary reasons." I bank my hopes on this school being a little more gracious.

Indeed, there is a phone, along with a couple of cracked couches, some Formica-covered tables, several hard chairs, and a fridge. No one else is in the room, yet. It shouldn't have mattered; I am making a legitimate call, but it did matter. For some reason, I want to be alone when I talk to Lydia.

I pick up the phone and dial the number I'd memorized yesterday. When her smooth voice comes on the line, I almost hang up. What was it about her that reduces me to a pimply faced teen with his first crush?

"Hello," she says.

"Ummm…Ms. Hawthorne," I stammer. "This is Mr. Burns, David's English teacher."

"Oh. David talks about you all the time." Present tense, interesting. She's sure he's coming back.

"Madison told me about your plans for this afternoon. I thought an extra pair of hands would help, if that's okay with you."

"Of course, it's okay with me. That would be great." Her words are happy, but her tone isn't. She is on the verge of tears.

Don't ask. Don't ask. Don't—"What's wrong?"

"Nothing. It's okay. Do you want to meet in the lobby?" It is the perfect opportunity for her to dump on me, but she doesn't do it. She goes up another notch in my book. Plus, I'd dodged a bullet—no kryptonite tears today.

"Lobby's good. Why don't I drive?"

"Okay sure, I'll see you then."

I don't want to hang up. I frantically search for a reason to continue the call. "Have you thought about where you want to go?"

"The park, the library, and everywhere in between."

"That narrows it down," I say.

She chuckles briefly. "The police are doing a good job, but they have other cases. I just want..." she pauses. I can hear the quiver in her voice. When she continues, her tone is even again. "I don't want to miss anything."

She's one tough chick. The thought bothers me. While on one hand I respect her strength, on the other I want to be strong *for* her. I want to be able to tell her everything will be okay and mean it. I want to fix it for her. But I can't. I'm not that guy. I am here today and gone tomorrow.

"We'll do what we can," I say. "See you this afternoon."

"Okay. I'm printing more flyers now. I should have them ready by two."

We exchange goodbyes and hang up. I realize why I didn't want anyone in the room—when I talk to her, I'm the closest I've been to myself in 779 days.

Fourth period. "What happened to your hand?"

"Zombie apocalypse. Don't worry I wasn't bitten."

Maddie is in this class, so I leave out the David talk. I don't want her to hear all those silly rumors. Madds, along with the rest of the class, is more insightful and engaged than the other groups so far. I almost have fun. Before I know it, the bell is ringing.

Fifth period. "Reavers." One geek gets it. I have to explain it to everyone else. No one knows anything useful about David, not that I am surprised. I keep asking, though, because I'd made a deal. We don't get far into the lesson before the lunch bell rings. What genius schedules lunch in the middle of fifth period?

I watch the delinquents go off to eat, and then I wander to the break room. When I come in, most teachers are already seated. One table holds Mrs. Watson and two other women, chatting away. The other table holds two bored men reading the paper. I eavesdrop on the women as I am nuking my Manly Appetites Frozen Glop.

"…and they were tossing her tampon around the room," the woman sitting next to Watson says, shaking her head.

Watson chuckles and answers, "Jerry Johnson actually told me he had a yeast infection, and that's why he was going to the bathroom so much."

All three erupt into giggles. The timer on the microwave dings, and I sit at the guy table, still within watching and listening distance.

"I don't know why you still do it, Susan. It's not like you have to," the first woman says. Mrs. Watson's face goes pale despite her flawless make-up, and she begins twisting her ring feverishly. The first woman's hand flies to her mouth, and then to Watson's arm. "I'm so sorry. That was so insensitive. I didn't mean—"

"It's okay," Watson interrupts. "It's true. Warren made sure I'd be okay after he was gone." Twist, twist. "I just can't imagine sitting around the house all day or going to the club. I don't relate with those women. I guess as long as the good days outweigh the bad, I'll keep teaching."

"Warren was such a great man. All that work he sponsored on the stadium and the new uniforms. What a benefit he was to this school," the second woman says. The first nods in agreement.

Watson keeps twisting her ring. "You must miss him every day," the second woman adds.

Mr. King walks in at that moment, winning the all-time prize for bad timing. He glances at Watson with the same heat he had that morning and says, "Hello, Mrs. Watson. Doris, Angela."

The other two women smile and mutter, "Hello, Ryan."

Watson barely spares him a glance before looking away and resuming her ring twisting. I wonder if she might sever her finger from all the friction. Mr. King is clearly not pleased by the rebuff. Anger, followed quickly by hurt, races across his handsome face. He marches to the fridge, pulls out one of those vitamin-laden waters, chugs half of it, and leaves the room. Watson watches him go, then looks back down at the table.

I am so caught up in the whole scene; all I can do is observe. My mind only has room to register what is going on before me. Once it is over though, my head buzzes. I was *wrong*. Let's not get carried away. Technically, I was right. Watson is having an affair about which she feels guilty. There is also a loving husband that provides her with jewels and designer clothes. I am only mistaken about one small, practically insignificant fact—said husband is dead. Watson is not the adulterous hag I originally presumed her to be.

I am rocked. I've never been wrong, er mistaken, before. I am Smullian. I'm the best. I don't screw up. Technically, I must point out again, I didn't screw up. The information was accurate. My interpretation of said information was skewed. That fact doesn't appease me. My interpretations drive everything I do. Who I con and who I don't, who I associate with or don't—my entire life is founded on my interpretation of the facts.

I squirm in my chair. A million needles crawl up and down my spine. I resist the next thought as long as I can, but it comes gushing forth like a broken dam. How many people have I conned that didn't deserve it? I can't help but wonder about all those marks whose money has passed my palm. How many of them are like Watson? How many have appeared one way, but were really another?

Suddenly, my glop isn't so appetizing. Okay, it wasn't appetizing to begin with, but now I can't imagine putting another sporkful in my mouth. I am a criminal, but I've always prided myself on being one with principles—kind of like Robin Hood, only I keep the money because I'm the poor that needs it. *Am I just another crook?* My stomach rolls like I am biotransposing, and I rush into the bathroom.

I don't need to use the john. I need time to think. Once I have some privacy, I immediately calm down. What are the chances of that happening more than once? A bazillion to one? This is a freak coincidence, nothing more. If anything, I've learned to carefully research my marks once I am back on the take. That's it. No life-altering revelations. I've shown *him*. It'll take a lot more than that to bring down Smullian O'Toole. It bothers me, though. Why does the Interloper care if I feel bad about my crimes? I know why The Powers-that-Be at Life Mod care, but they aren't currently driving this ship. The Interloper is setting my schedule and, as far as I know, he cares about David. What does it matter to him if I develop a conscience?

I am amazed at my own paranoia. This is what the last three days have reduced me to—talking out loud to people who aren't there and seeing conspiracy behind every coincidence. This whole situation amounts to one large coincidence like the Ferrari being stolen. The situation with Watson and King was already going on. I noticed it because I'm that good, not for any other reason. Get a grip, Smullian.

When I leave the bathroom, I notice that Watson is gone. Maybe her finger fell off and she is reattaching it. More likely she needed privacy, as well. I dump my glop, make some comment about grading papers, and head back to class. When I pass Watson's room, I hear her talking to someone that could only be Mr. King. It is obvious this isn't the first time they'd had this discussion.

"Is it wrong of me to want to share lunch *with* my girl?"

"No, Ryan," Watson says. "I just need a little more time."

"We've been together six months, Susan. How much more time do you want?"

"I don't, I don't know," she stammers. "Doris was talking about—"

"I don't give a rip what Doris or anyone else says. The last I checked, they weren't part of this relationship. I know Warren was a saint, but he's been gone two years. I'm starting to wonder if you're ashamed of me."

"Ryan, it's not like that. Of course, I'm not…Please, be patient."

"Yeah well, I don't have that much patience left." I sense the end of the conversation, and scoot to my room. *Six months. Wow. He must be deeply into her.* Poor Watson, not only was she battling her own guilt about moving on, but everyone else's thoughts on the matter. I make it to my desk just as King storms past in a haze of manly fury. I don't blame him—I'd be raging too. Yet another reason I choose to stay footloose and fancy free—no one has control over my emotions but me.

The lunch bell chimes, and the inmates return. It takes forever to calm them down, and by then we only have a few more moments for discussion. I again curse the mouth-breather who scheduled lunch in the middle of class.

"I feel sorry for Shylock," says a girl wearing a peasant blouse. She has no makeup and sports long dangly earrings. I am willing to bet my life she is a vegetarian. No doubt she is one of those idealistic youths that spend all their time commenting on the world's troubles, which is a luxury only afforded to people who've never experienced any real problems.

"Why is that?" I ask.

"Well, people have been mean to him his whole life. They pick on him and treat him badly. He's not a bad guy. He's just trying to make it in a harsh world."

"Are you nuts?" barks a student from the back of the room. "If he gets that pound of flesh, Antonio will die. That's murder."

"Let's keep our discussion civil—no insults," I say, pointing to the offender while inwardly agreeing with the assessment. "Let me ask it this way, do you feel that Shylock's rough life justifies his being a criminal—that it makes all of his crimes okay?"

At that moment, the bell rings, silencing all further discussion. The question hangs heavy in the room. I try to avoid it by busying myself at Burnsey's desk. It doesn't work. The question is there, and it needs an answer. In the context of the class discussion, the answer is, "Of course not. Having a rough life doesn't justify criminal behavior." But in the context of my life, it is my reigning philosophy.

For the second time in less than an hour, I am confronted with the notion that I may not be perfect. The barricade holding back my anger threatens to tumble. I want to repeat this morning's temper tantrum, but poor Burnsey's hands can only take so much. What right does this Interloper have coming in and messing with my life? I was quite happy before he came along. What is he trying to accomplish? Well, I'd made a deal to help with David; I didn't make one to grow a conscience. No one is in the room, so I steal a quick glance upward and say, "I help with David. *That's* the deal." There isn't a response.

The events of the last hour have put me in a dark mood. I stare at my desk and tap a pen with the ferocity of a nerpes perforating a rock. I take a deep breath, hold it, and expel it with force. This day sucks. This whole week sucks. I doubt I have the energy to put on the show for yet another set of delinquents.

IV

I hear them coming in, but don't bother to look up. I am so not in the mood. I ignore the heathens and keep banging away with my pen. The unmistakable screech of a metal chair being dragged across the floor grabs my attention. I glance up. I'm going to have to acknowledge the little punks soon anyway.

The room has been transformed. One student has repositioned two desks, so that he can sit at one while propping his feet on the other. A group of girls have arranged their desks in a circle. One kid is sitting cross-legged on the floor with his back against the wall. The odd seating configuration isn't the only break with normal class protocol. Several students are slurping sodas or crunching chips.

Since all the students are involved, not just one rebellious kid, I have to assume that Keith's usual rules don't apply. I decide on a quick test.

"What is the rule about food in my class?" I bark at a nearby girl.

She pauses mid-munch and says, "Only if we give you some."

"That's right," I answer with a chuckle.

She hops up and shakes a few nacho chips free from her bag onto the desk. To my surprise, several other students follow her lead. Soon I have a smorgasbord of junk food—three kinds of chips, some popcorn, and a cookie. This is an excellent hustle. I'm kind of proud of Burnsey.

Obviously, this class is different. Why? I look at the schedule. Last period is listed as Creative Writing. The words cause a slight panic. I had only checked out the one lesson plan. It didn't occur to me that Keith would teach more than one subject. Between the *Exhaustive Lexicon* and my own experiences spinning yarns, I know quite a bit about fiction. But I don't know what aspect they're covering in class.

"What happened to your hand?" asks a perky girl in the aforementioned circular gaggle of females. Whew. I'm saved by a well-timed question.

"That's today's assignment." I smile. "I'm going to write several explanations for this injury on the board. Choose the scenario that most inspires you and write that story."

I write out all the excuses I've been using all day, from home repair accident to Reaver attack. Surprisingly, no one asks what a Reaver is. Either they already know, or being creative, they've painted a description from their own imaginations. I think I might actually like these kids. I hear gasps and grunts, the auditory expressions of their storytelling gears grinding to life. Even without looking, I know they are excited about the assignment.

When I finish writing out the story prompts, I turn to find several already hunched over their notebooks, some paper and some digital, writing. Others are gazing off into space as they mentally work out the story. One boy tilts his head from side to side, lost in his own internal conversation.

Seeing their little minds whirring as they eagerly approach an assignment I gave them is a rush. This must be why Burnsey does it. A person could put up with a lot of flarp, if there were moments when he knew he was making an impact. Last week, I wouldn't have felt this way. I'd have mocked Keith for needing this kind of affirmation. A man should be footloose, fancy free, and definitely not need the validation of a bunch of mindless, adolescent zombies. That's what I would have thought. Now I'm sitting here all jazzed 'cause some twerps are engaged by something I did. What's next? Crying at chick flicks? I blame David for the mess I'm in. Little twerp.

This thought reminds me that I'm supposed to ask each class about David. I could let it go. It's not like the questions has yielded any useful information today. Besides, I hate to interrupt the creative flow these kids are in. However, I made a deal, and I don't welch. I have rules.

"Before you get too far into your stories, I need to ask you about David Hawthorne." I wait for the ridiculous half-truths and rumors.

"What happened to him?" a girl asks. "Madison is really upset."

"People are saying the stupidest things," another chimes in.

I am surprised, but I shouldn't be. Of course, these artists, these teens that don't fit the mold, would know David.

"We're not entirely sure," I answer. "The police are looking for information. Did any of you see or talk to him on Sunday or Monday?"

"I saw him on Monday," says the boy sitting on the floor. He's dressed in head to toe black like he'd hit a fire sale at "Goths R Us."

"Where?"

"At the gas station. Mom was making me pump. He walked into the store. I thought he was ditching class."

"What time was that?"

He fiddled with the stud in his lip. "It was after my doctor appointment. Maybe 10 or 10:30."

Finally, some helpful information. I'd pat myself on the back if that wouldn't draw unwanted attention. I did it. I played ball. The Father will have no choice but to honor our deal now. Pool boy, here I come. I beckon to Goth Guy.

"Why don't the rest of you get back to your stories while we go call the detective handling the case?"

I'd be worried about leaving another class unattended, but these guys actually want to work. Hopefully, this information will be enough to break the case open. I don't want my tour in the Caribbean serving scantily clad women who have been drinking too many cocktails in the hot sun to be tainted by worry over Lydia. I guess I'm worried about the twerp, too. I know first-hand how mean the streets are and, while I managed to survive, I wouldn't want to wish that experience on anyone, especially not a sweet kid like David.

I usher Goth Guy down to the teacher's lounge. I bet Burnsey still has Benigno's card in his wallet. Keith's optimistic enough to believe he might have an opportunity to use it. I flip open the wallet and dig through. Sure enough, the card is tucked under the credit cards.

I dial the number and wait. I'm a little nervous. I've never communicated with someone I've brain-hitched before. It's the ultimate test. His partner and his wife bought my act, but now I'll be able to compare myself with the original.

"Missing Persons. Detective Diaz."

"This is Keith Burns. David Hawthorne's English teacher. I have a student who saw David on Monday morning."

"Good. Can I interview him?" Perfunctory and professional— just like I played him. You are the best, Smullian O'Toole.

"I have him here now, if a phone interview is okay."

"Yes. Put him on the line."

I hand the phone over, giving the boy a reassuring smile. "Just tell the detective what you told me."

From listening to the kid's side of the conversation, I figure Benny Boy went over the story with him three times. Each time, Diaz skillfully coaxed out additional details. David had his backpack. David waved. David was smiling. David walked in the direction of a nearby bus stop.

It's strange that David waved. When you are running away, you don't want to attract unwanted attention. If you can't back away or change direction when you see someone you know, you keep your head down and mosey on like you didn't see him. You don't slap on a grin and wave. This information, combined with the fact that he didn't leave Lydia a note, makes me uneasy. If he hadn't stolen the Rock the Universe money, I'd say something bad had happened. All I can be sure of now is that things aren't as cut and dried as I originally thought.

After Goth Guy is finished, I get back on the line. "I hope this helps."

"It shores up the timeline," Benny answers.

"Lydia, Madison, and I are going to hang flyers this afternoon."

"Good. Every little bit helps."

I'm not sure if he means it. The chip in my brain tells me that tip lines and public appeals lead to a plethora of crackpots blaming aliens and Jimmy Hoffa. Police work is doubled or tripled running down specious information. I feel bad for the increased workload, but I told the girls I'd help. Besides, I understand that for them, hanging flyers gives a sense of control in an otherwise maddening situation. I'd give anything for Lydia to feel better, even for a few minutes.

Yep. Bring on the chick flicks. I've reached full-on sap level.

The call ends, and I escort Goth Guy back to class. As I predicted, the little urchins are jotting away so lost in their imagined worlds that they don't even look up when I reenter the room. Too soon, the bell rings. Some scoot out, but a few linger on eking out the last few precious sentences before they have to catch the bus.

I give 'em five and clear my throat. I admit that I'm enjoying their eagerness to work, but Lydia is waiting. I'm nervous and excited like I'm sixteen or something waiting for a first date. Or what I imagine it would be like. There wasn't so much dating for me as there were random, heated, desperate hook ups in dark, seedy places. When you're constantly on the move and everyone is about what they can get from you, there really isn't room for true connections. Anyway, these kiddos need to move on. I have somewhere to be.

V

Just to be clear, everything still sucks. But the last class did pull me out of the muck for fifty minutes, and, for that, I am slightly less irritated by how things have been going. I may have to spend the next few hours assuaging the fears of two emotional females, but I also get to appreciate how nicely Lydia fills out her jeans. There's nothing wrong with enjoying the scenery, as Chuckles says. I've been good. I've played ball. The Father better honor our bargain. Tomorrow I will be in the Caribbean, and all this mess will be far behind me.

You can't keep me down for long. I'm a survivor. Mood elevated, I pack up and saunter down the hall. That's when I see Mrs. Watson. She's sitting at her desk, staring out into the aether, and twisting the neth out of that ring. I was joking about her severing her finger earlier, but now I have some genuine concern about the fate of that digit. Her uptight, perfect posture bows under the eighteen tons of guilt she has placed upon herself.

Walk on by, Smullian my boy. This is not your job. Your job is that little twerp. No one else expects any more of you than that, and you don't owe anyone more than that. This is not your problem.

I stop anyway. It's not my problem, but at the same time I want to help. *I* want to help. I'm wavering here in Watson's doorway not because it's something I think Keith would do, which he would—annoying good guy. But because I am compelled to do something to ease her pain. *Drak.*

I awkwardly clear my throat. Watson adjusts her posture and plants a well-rehearsed smile on her face. "What do you need, Keith?"

I do the patented Burnsey cheek blow out and stammer, "I, uh, heard, uh, you and Ryan earlier."

Equal parts terror and sorrow cover her face. "You did?"

"Yeah and I, uh, wanted to tell you that, uh, I think Warren would want you to be happy. If I were him, that's what I'd want. People aren't supposed to mourn forever. Those of us still around owe it to those that, uh, aren't…to enjoy our lives. And I, uh, think those people who, uh, care about you want the same thing. Those that don't should stick it."

She chuckles. Well, that's being generous. It isn't more than a quiet expulsion of air, but it's a step in the right direction. "That's what you think?"

"Yeah. You and Ryan make a good couple."

"Thank you."

Raw, unfettered gratitude emanates from her face. It terrifies me. I want to run. I want to restore the wall I've built around myself brick by brick. The last thing I desire is to be caught in this vulnerable moment with her. But I can't run. I have to stand here and take it. Her eyes radiate warmth, joy, and a bittersweet sadness. The utter humanness of this connection is overwhelming, and I think I may drown in it.

"You're a good man, Keith."

Keith, yes, but not me. Her statement burns like an accusation. I clear my throat and make ready to escape.

Before I can go, she adds one last dagger. "And a good friend."

I cut a fast clip down the hall, around the corner, and into the stairwell. I lean against the wall, attempting to gather myself before I face the girls. *A good friend.* What a joke. Smullian O'Toole does not have friends. For me, people fall into one of two categories: those I can rip off, and those I can use. I guess that sounds cynical, but no one has ever done me any favors. Why should I do any for them? Life is a series of contracts. You do this for me; I do this for you. It's all about barter of goods, exchange of services. Food, shelter, transportation, sex. These things are inherent needs with inherent values attached to them. I provide something of equal worth, and I get my needs met.

The concept that someone out there will feed you because they "like" you is irrational. You can't quantify a feeling. Emotions are as changeable as the wind, and so are the people that have them. What happens when they don't like you anymore? When they're angry? When they die? I'll tell you what happens. You're left cold, hungry, and alone.

Friendship is a myth that fades under the harsh light of reality. But…yesterday, I saw an example that didn't fade when real life reared its head. Chuckles got mad at Benny, er, me, but instead of bailing, he forgave. By the time we reached the car, all was well. But I digress.

I've got one very fine woman and a good kid waiting for me downstairs. There's a perfect example of my life philosophy. I'm helping the girls because I get something from it. Exchange of services. I'm only hanging flyers to get out of this crazy fix I'm in.

Or am I?

My heart literally skips a beat when I see Lydia. Her golden hair is up in a ponytail, which usually isn't my thing I like a girl's hair down and flowing, but with hers up I can better make out her features. Each time I see her I'm surprised by how lovely she is. Her jawline and cheekbones are smoothly etched, defined, but not harsh or pointy. Even without the benefit of eyeliner and shadow, her blue eyes sparkle. But really, she's more than the sum of her various parts—her internal sweetness somehow shines through escalating her beauty.

Ugh. Seriously, I'm gushing about her inner beauty like a Hallmark card. Actually, having her around would have been helpful on Day 264 when I was stuck writing Hallmark cards.

I look down at the floor to gain control and pull on Burnsey again. Another second and I'll be drooling all over her, which would be inappropriate because her brother is missing. I don't think she's interested in hearing how beautiful she is at this juncture, especially not from a frumpy teacher at least twelve years her senior.

As the three of us walk to my car, I fill the girls in on Goth Guy's insight about David. Lydia wants to go to the gas station first. I'm not sure what she expects. She's not going to find him there, and I doubt the structure will be giving off psychic vibes about his location. Benny and Chuckles have the gas station covered; it's a much better use of our valuable time and resources to check out other locations. Lydia doesn't see my logic. *Just like a girl, eschew rational thought for a feeling. Oh well, it's not my dime.* I'm supposed to play ball, and saying we'll go makes her happy. I like seeing her happy, although I'm scared of the fallout that is inevitable. Each passing day means it's less likely we'll find David or increases the likelihood we'll find his body.

What am I thinking? I don't want to claim that doom just yet, even if it is realistic. When, and if, that does happen I'm glad I'll be long gone. Seeing Lydia's world collapse would break my heart. I'm glad I'll be gone tomorrow; I want to remember her the way she looks right now: hope sparkling in her eyes, determination in her jaw.

We hit the gas station and run into Benny and Chuckles. There is some awkward intercourse before they fill us in on what they've got.

"We just finished reviewing the security footage. David was here at 10:37 AM. He paid cash, but we could tell he bought two bottles of Gatorade and what looked like a cigarette lighter." Benny concludes perfunctorily, closing his notebook with a sharp snap. *That's exactly how I would have played it. Surreal.*

"He loves Gatorade," Lydia says. Then a guilty downward cast of her eyes as she adds, "We can only buy it when it's on sale."

"Does he smoke?" Chuckles asks.

"No," the girls bark in unison.

"That's kind of a strange purchase. I wonder what he needed it for," I mutter, but don't add that a source of fire is invaluable when you're on the run. One can't always find shelter, and you might need to sleep or eat outdoors. I don't think this information will soothe Lydia or Madds, so I keep my yap shut.

"Our witness said he headed over to that bus stop, so we're over to JTA next to find out which route that is and check for security footage on the bus," says Benny.

We part ways, but Lydia still wants to look inside. Maybe she is trying to channel her brother. The convenience store is clean and neat, yet still has that vague odor of old hot dogs and Slurpees that all of these establishments exhibit despite the state of repair. We walk to the front where we discover that the 32 oz Gatorades are buy one, get one free.

"He wouldn't have been able to resist this," Lydia says, picking one up. "I bet he bought orange and blue." She's cradling the bottle as if she were holding a Ming vase instead of some clunky plastic. Maddie picks one up as well. It's like the bottles are hypnotizing them. The lighters are next to the register on the counter, decorated with different logos: cowboy hats, race cars, skulls. Maddie snatches up the one with the skulls.

"I bet he bought one like this." Then she grabs one with smiley faces. "Or he might have bought this one because it was ironic."

I guess I get it. This is the last place David was seen. For both of them, it's a link to him. Like Stonehenge, the store holds a connection to the past, and they hope lingering there will help them conjure him up. It won't. David isn't here anymore. He hasn't been here for two-and-half days. I lay my hand on Lydia's shoulder. This is the first time I've consciously touched her. Her smooth skin feels warm and soft. Suddenly, I don't know what to do with my hand. Is it comforting or pervy? Do I leave it there or move it? I resist the urge to yank it off her shoulder because that would definitely be weird.

"We should head on," I say, removing my hand at what I hope is a normal, uncreepy speed. Lydia clutches the bottle a moment longer, then puts it back in the display. As she's done so many times in the past two days, she sheds her sorrow and clothes her herself with resolve.

"Come on, Em. We've got work to do," she proclaims and heads out to the car.

She's already given Madds a nickname. They're already bonding. For most people, a nickname is a sign of affection. For me, it's about the job. Nicknames are a quick way to remember people's attributes and foibles, what makes them an easy target. They are not terms of endearment. Using nicknames also keeps people at bay. If I never call a person by their name, I keep them dehumanized; they are not people, just caricatures.

Huh, once I learned Lydia's name, that's all I've called her. I wonder what the shrinks at Life Mod would think that means.

We decide to canvass the strip center across from the gas station. There are several stores there, and we hope someone saw him. It's also a good vantage place for flyers because it's near both the gas station and the bus stop. The first few stores yield no leads, but they let us put flyers in their windows. Finally, the lady at the Hallmark store recognizes him.

"Yeah, I saw that kid. He was waiting at the door when I opened the shop. Real eager beaver. Bought all of my white pillars."

"What?" Lydia asks.

The lady walks us over to the candle section of the store. The scent of wax and vanilla assaults our noses.

"He bustles right in and clears me out of my white pillars, five of them. He bought a red one, too. I figured he needed them for some sort of school project. Real nice boy. Paid in cash, then left."

"Did you see where he went?" I ask.

"Nope, I had another customer." We ask her to retell the story three more times, but she doesn't have any more information.

When we explain that he is missing, she expresses sorrow, "Shame. He was such a handsome boy. Real polite. Why don't you hang that up in our window?"

Candles? Candles are weird. Everything else he's done makes sense in light of running off, but pillar candles are heavy and unwieldy. They'd only slow him down. Plus, he had to know there'd be flashlights at the convenience store. Why buy six candles when one flashlight is cheaper and lighter? *Not your problem, Smullian. Gone tomorrow, remember? This is not your mystery to solve. Aren't you happy about that?* Despite the odd purchase, the girls are buoyed by the exchange. They drag me into every business in the surrounding area, but no luck.

"Why don't we go to the park? He loves it there," Maddie suggests.

"I'm not sure what good that would do. We know he was here Monday morning. The park's ten minutes down the road," I answer, feeling a little like Debbie Downer.

"Mrs. Granger heard him leave at 6:45, but he wasn't here until the store opened at 10. Where did he go in between? He might have gone to the park."

"Makes sense, Em," Lydia says. Then she looks authoritatively at me. "Let's go."

Is it wrong that I like so much when she gets feisty? I shrug and exhale, Burnsey-style. "I guess it's logical."

We all pile back into the car and head to the park. No one's talking. It's dawned on the girls that while we've gotten more information, we're no closer to an answer. In fact, the more we learn, the more perplexing his disappearance becomes. I turn on the radio to dispel the silence.

Unlike the funereal car ride, the park is alive. A couple of moms chat while their offspring dash around the playground with shouts and giggles. A few fitness nuts in bright, tight clothing jog down the nature trail. Fishermen lean over the end of a recently stained dock, casting into the sparkling St. John's River. I smell burning charcoal and turn to see a family prepping in the pavilion for a picnic dinner. I see why David likes it here. He can be in the presence of people without having to interact with them. It's a place where he can quietly observe life as he scratches out sketches in his book.

We show his picture to several patrons to no avail. One gentleman does recognize David as a park regular but hadn't seen him in more than a week. While we're canvassing, a young woman enters the picnic area. I should say "enters stage left" because that's how it feels, like a production. Her dark locks are pulled back with a gauzy, beaded scarf. Her long skirt, also beaded, is a wild array of colors. Her shirt a ruffled mess. I hear a faint tinkling of bells; it's a bracelet—no, an anklet. I'm certain of it. The whole outfit screams, "Look at me! I'm bohemian." But it's all wrong.

The arrangement of the scarf on her head is too perfectly placed, with flattering loose, dark tendrils of hair framing her face. The skirt and shirt, meant to appear disheveled as if the wearer cared not at all for trivial things such as appearance, still shows off her slender figure, and the colors complement her copper skin, dark hair, and raven eyes. I catch the faint hint of floral fragrance in the air, which goes against a true hippie's love of all-natural hygiene products that do little to curb body odor.

My blood starts to boil. There is one type of small-time crook I loathe. They don't even deserve to be called grifters. They're con men, plain and simple. Mediums. In confirmation of my suspicions, she climbs onto one of the tables with her anklet jingling along in accompaniment. She elaborately waves her arms about, and then rests them in the classic meditation position. She aggressively shakes her head from side to side, loudly inhaling and exhaling. Then, she proceeds to meditate. All of this, from her elaborate dress to her theatric posing, is designed to draw all eyes to her. As I said, a production. This isn't a gentle soul communing with the elements. This is a spider weaving her web. *Did David fall into it?*

I've known a few psychics/mediums in my journeys, and I assure you they're all the same. They are cold-blooded, heartless invertebrates ready to maximize a person's tragedy by bilking them for every penny they've got. I consider them the bottom of the heap not only because I would never take advantage of someone's suffering just to make a buck, but also because it's a waste of talent. This type of scam requires someone be adept at cold reading and aware of a person's physical cues, body language, and even breath speed to determine facts about them. We tell our life stories to people every day without saying a single word. Psychics can pick up on all that. It takes phenomenal observational skill, and they waste it on low-hanging fruit. It's easy to con someone in the throes of grief; they want to believe loved ones are out there waiting to talk to them. Bilking a love-starved person? They've done half the work for you. They've already deluded themselves that there's a special someone out there. Being a psychic or medium is lazy, as well as dastardly, as far as I'm concerned.

A sensitive, guilt-ridden boy would be easy prey to a witch like this. She makes my spidey sense tingle. I glance over at Lydia and Madds. They're busy talking to the family at the pavilion. I don't want them with me when I talk to this fraud. She'll try to snare them. I shuffle over to her table, which is centrally located for maximum visibility.

"Have you seen this boy?" I say, holding up the flyer.

She glances at it. "I've never seen this young man."

She closes her eyes and returns to her "meditation." It's a deliberate dismissal. She doesn't want to look at the picture or talk to me. I tap her on the leg and hold the photo inches from her nose. "Are you sure? David comes to this park regularly."

She practically slaps my hand away. "No, I'd remember such a noble child. I commune here with the spirits daily."

As I've already mentioned, we nefarious types do well because we dehumanize our victims. I want her to look at him; I want her to hear his name. I want him to be real to her. I put the flyer in her lap. "Well, thank you Miss, uh," I stammer, waiting for her to fill in her name. Not that I think it will actually be her name.

"Bronwen Evangelista." *What gothic romance did she rip that from?*

"Keep the flyer. Call the number at the bottom, if the spirits tell you anything about David." I tap the photo, bringing attention again to his face.

"Certainly, nothing would please me more than to help this poor soul," she says as she picks up the flyer and places it facedown beside her on the table.

Three things are painfully evident: 1) she's a con man 2) she's lying 3) she knows something about David's disappearance. I resist the urge to grab her by the throat and squeeze until she coughs up what she knows, but I can't risk it. *Bodily harm to another while in a host? I have no idea what that would do to my sentence. I'm scared for the kid. This is bad, but I can't risk alternative sentencing for the twerp. There's too much time already under my belt to mess it up now. I'll call Benny boy. He'll handle it. It's his area anyway.*

I take one last stab at humanizing him for her. "Are you sure you don't know anything? That's David's sister and girlfriend. David's been missing since Monday, and I'm sure you can imagine what torture it is for the two of them. They'd give anything to have David back home. David's only 15."

Bronwen's face is tight, and her eyes glazed over. She's steeling herself against the guilt. "No," she says with forced civility. "I've never seen this lad."

I storm off before I do something that will be vastly satisfying, but regretful. I debate telling Lydia. If I do, she might march over there and rip into our psychic fraud. I fear I pushed it too far, and, if Lydia gets added to the mix, Bronwen might skip out before Benny can get his hooks into her. But I can't lie to Lydia. I lie to women multiple times a day; it's never been any sweat off my brow. They lie to me. I lie to them. We all get what we want. I don't want to do that with Lydia…which is really kind of comical, because since I've met her, I've pretended to be three different people she knows. I've perpetrated an immense charade on her, but an outright lie? I can't do it.

I gather her and Maddie close and whisper, "That woman knows something. She's lying. Don't go over there. Detective Diaz should interview her. It could be nothing. I think she's a con artist; she may not want to say what she knows because it will expose her own crimes. She may not know anything important, but she is lying."

"How do you know?" Lydia whispers.

"Trust me, I know. Let's go to the car, and I'll call Detective Diaz."

I catch up with Diaz, fill him in on the Hallmark lady, and then tell him about Bronwen.

"She said she hadn't seen him. Doesn't seem like much of a lead." He sounds distracted.

"I've been a teacher a long time. She is definitely lying. I've learned to recognize the signs."

"If we have time, we'll swing by tomorrow and interview her."

He's coddling me. I press. "Even if she doesn't know anything about David, I'd have someone keep an eye on her for fraud. She's all kinds of shady. She said her name was Bronwen Evangelista, though I doubt that's on a birth certificate anywhere."

"Thank you. We'll follow-up on the Hallmark store and this woman at the park." The call ends. I resist beating the phone into the dashboard, refraining for the benefit of the girls. I know he's doing his job. I know he and Chuckles are beating down every lead. I know they have their concerns about the runaway angle. But I'm still irritated. *Doesn't he get it? This could be so much worse than we first thought*

VI

Next stop, local library. Lydia and Madds erupt from the car like they're strapped in ejection seats. Flyers in hand, they are ready for another round.

"You girls go on," I call after them. "I need to connect with a parent." It's not an outright lie; Benny will be a parent soon. I can't help it if the girls assume I meant a student's parent.

Lydia nods in agreement and leads Maddie inside. *I need to try again. He **has** to understand.* I dial.

"Detective Diaz," the voice answers.

"Uh…This is Keith Burns again. I have some concerns I don't want to share where Lydia can hear."

"I assure you. Detective Weidman and I are doing all we can to—"

"Gosh no. I'm not concerned about how you're doing your jobs. I'm concerned about David. I didn't think he'd run away in the first place." I talk fast, so Benny Boy can't get a chance to interrupt. "Now these candles. That's not a typical thing to buy when you're running off. They make no sense. What possible reason could David have for them? I think it means he wasn't planning on taking off. He was skipping school for something, but not leaving town. That's why there wasn't a note. Whatever he was doing with the money didn't have to do with splitting. Second, that chick Bronwen's possible involvement has chills running up my spine. She gave me the creeps. What if she's a scout? Looking for young, vulnerable boys and girls without much family for…you know…nefarious purposes. What if David is right now trapped in a sex trafficking ring?" *It almost happened to me once, but I was road-wise enough to catch on before they lowered the boom. David is sweet and trusting; perfect meat for a scam like that.*

"Believe me, Mr. Burns. We are covering Every. Possible. Angle. Even the painful and frightening ones. We want to bring David home safe and sound. I get you're scared. I'm glad you shared this with me and not Lydia. She doesn't need any added stress. I doubt this possibility has crossed her mind."

"I hope it never does."

"Your mouth to god's ears," Diaz says with a light chuckle. "I know you feel useless right now, but you being there for Lydia does more than you know. Plus, I don't know if you believe in prayer, but I do. David can use every bit he can get. The Bible says the prayer of a righteous man avails much." *Righteous? That word may describe Burnsey, but definitely not me.*

I glance up and notice the girls walking out of the library.

"Lydia is coming. I need to go." I hang up as they approach the car. *Talking to Diaz accomplished nothing. I don't feel any better. I'm not sure what I was hoping for. Benny hit the nail on the head. "Useless," that's what I am. Impotent's an even better word. What is the Father thinking? What has all this frantic running around today achieved except a weighted stone slowly sinking down my throat?*

"The librarian recognized him," Maddie reports, breaking me from my self-pitying thoughts. "But hasn't seen him since this weekend. She let us hang up the flyers, though. Do you mind taking me home? Mom texted and says its time."

"Sure, no problem."

I drop Madds at home and, once again, I'm alone with Lydia. I want to hold onto my time with her as long as possible. It's completely selfish. There's so much on her mind, but after today I'll be gone. I won't ever see her again. It kills me to admit it; I want more of her.

"Have you eaten today?"

"A little. Mrs. Granger brought me over some sweet rolls. Very thoughtful of her. Although…I haven't been that hungry."

"You should eat whether you want to or not. I bet you're not sleeping well. You need the energy and stuff." *Argh. Stuff, really! He's an English teacher. I'm sure he could come up with a more sophisticated word than stuff.* "Let me buy some supper before you head home."

"Okay. I'm not ready to go back there anyway. It's too empty. Too quiet, without David."

"Don't you have friends or church people coming by?"

"Most of my friends graduated, moved away. Those who are still here live way out beachside. I work so much. We haven't really been able to get connected in a church. David won't go without me."

"Sounds lonely."

"I'm too tired to notice," she says blithely.

How does she stay so positive?

We hit up a local pizza place called Al's. It's too late for the lunch crowd and too early for the dinner rush, so we have the place to ourselves. Normally, I would hate the quiet. But I crave the chance to be alone with her, even if she thinks she's hanging with a chubby English teacher.

"What do you like?" I ask.

A shy smile crosses her face. "A little bit of everything. Dad used to call it 'Garbage Pizza.' But I'll eat whatever."

"A woman after my own heart." *I mean it. Food, one more thing we have in common.* The waitress stops by, and I order a large with everything and a couple of Cokes.

Lydia picks at her food at first, but once she has a few bites, exclaims, "I'm ravenous. I didn't realize how hungry I was." Then she really tucks in. Between bites, all of her pent- up worries come tumbling out.

"I don't resent it; the way things are. I really don't. Every once in a while, I wish things were better for both of us, but I love my brother. I love taking care of him. He's all I've got. Do you think he thought I resented him? Do you think I made him go?"

"It's obvious you've made a home for David. He knows that, too. If he ran away—and I'm not sure he did—it wasn't because he thought you didn't love him or want him. It's clear in everything you do for him. I have a friend whose mother died when he was quite young, twelve. He had no one. No family. No sister. I think he would have loved to have someone like you in his life."

"What did he do?"

"Bounced around from place to place."

"Foster care?"

"Something like that."

"How is he now?"

"Bitter and angry," I say with a grin, like I'm making a joke. "He's surviving."

"That's not much of a life, just surviving."

"No, it isn't. That's my point, though. David isn't just surviving with you. He has a life. You do things, plan concert trips. It's not an environment to run away from; it's an environment to run to."

"Things must be better for your friend now. He has you."

"Yeah," I say, sardonically. "I'm his only friend."

"Why doesn't he have more?"

"He has a hard time trusting people. He'd like you, I think."

"You should introduce us."

"He's not from around here." Sniff. "Oh, look at the time. I better get you home." A lost look envelops her face. *Nice one, Smullian. It got too real, so you had to be a jerk.*

"Are you sure there's no one who can stay with you?"

"No. Don't worry. I'll be okay. God is with me."

"How can you be so sure?"

"He hasn't failed me yet."

Has she lost her mind? I'm able to control my tone, but not my tongue. "How can you believe that after everything that's happened to you?"

"At first, I freaked out. Gut reaction. Then God sent me to Second Corinthians. Paul writes about how God comforts us during trials, so we can comfort others. After my parents and brother died, there were times the grief was so heavy I felt weighted to the bed. My muscles couldn't bear up under the load. It was God's strength that got me off that mattress, so that I could get David off his. It was just like Second Corinthians says. God comforted me; I comforted David. That experience is getting me through this one. I know God is there. He's carried me before; he's got me now."

"I don't think I'd see it that way. I'd be wondering why he let it happen to begin with."

"God's word doesn't say he prevents the bad stuff. It says he helps you through it. He's our strong tower and place of refuge. For him to be those things, must mean we need protection and refuge from something. I know for sure he's sheltered me through some pretty bad storms. God didn't make that car lose control, and whatever's going on with David, he's not behind that either. But he's right here beside me right now." She pauses and takes a sip from her soda. Then she looks at me with those penetrating blue eyes. "I'm kind of surprised you're asking these questions. David said you're a believer."

Good thing I am a master of excuses. "I was just playing devil's advocate, so you'd provide your own encouragement. It would sound pithy and cliché if I said those things."

"It worked. I do feel better. David is lost somewhere, but he's not alone. And neither am I."

Her logic confounds me. Her parents and brother have died. Her other brother is missing. She had to drop out of college and works at a flarppy diner, probably getting sexually harassed multiple times a day by truckers and Uber drivers. Yet she says *god* is with her? It's insane. I'd say god has abandoned her, if I believed in a concept as obtuse as a god.

We ride back to the school in a somewhat companionable silence. I drop her at her car, a sad, gray VW bug convertible that was cute in its younger days but is now long in the tooth and needing to be put out to pasture. She tosses her purse in the passenger seat and walks around the car. I watch her go, not ready to leave.

"Thanks for the help and the encouragement tonight," she says with that perfect smile. I try to memorize the contours of her face, the lilt of her voice. I'm going to be somewhere else tomorrow, and I'll never see her again. This morning getting the neth out of Jax was my number one goal, but not now. For the first time in 779 days, I don't want to be somewhere else tomorrow. I want to still be here in this flarppy town with these people. I give her a sort of half-salute, half-wave and roll on.

When I get home, I drop into bed, and I immediately think about David. The candles don't make sense, and Bronwen is a big red flag. I fear that he is somewhere alone, frightened, and in pain. As bad as my life was, I never had a situation like I believe David is in now. I had some tough breaks and close scrapes, but I made a way for myself. I guess Lydia would tag that as the support during the tough times. I'd say it was self-sufficiency and ingenuity on my part.

I wrestle my thoughts clear of David, only to have them land on Lydia. Yet another thing I have no power over. *Why me? What's the point? There is nothing I can do.*

"Father—" I jump from the bed and stalk to the bathroom.

"No, you are not going there, Smullian O'Toole. Have you lost your mind? Praying?" I dig through Burnsey's cabinets until find what I need. I gulp down half a bottle of Nyquil and head back to bed. Numb the thoughts, black out the dreams, and, hopefully, be rid of this whole situation tomorrow.

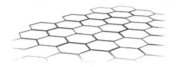

PART FOUR

PIT OF DESPAIR

I wake up and nausea, my old friend, yells for me to get going. I start to rise, but, when I move, pain explodes in my right leg. The sensation annihilates my thoughts, and only searing agony exists. After an eternity, it recedes. The stabbing after-shocks trigger my gag reflex, and I don't even have time to turn my head before I'm vomiting. Bile burns up my throat and out of my mouth and nose. There's not much of it and, pretty soon, I'm just dry heaving. The convulsions wake up other pains in my host's chest. I take ragged, shallow breaths because each intake awakens a new fresh hell in my torso. The nausea of biotransposition combined with the pain drives me to the edge of insanity. I grit my teeth and will them to stop. Caustic bile threatens to rise again. I fight it back, not wanting to set off more fireworks.

I'm not sure how long it takes, but the pain eventually dulls to throbs, and my nausea lessens to a manageable level. I am finally able to achieve some cogent thought and assess my situation. It feels like I'm in the bottom of a well. I can't say *looks* because I can't see anything. No light penetrates the blackness, and I have to fight an overwhelming sense of claustrophobia. I brace myself against the pain and produce a weak, "Hello?"

No one answers. I'm not surprised. Wherever I am, feels empty. I don't hear any scratches or skitters or hesitant breaths. The only sounds are mine. I am alone trapped in a pit somewhere, and there is no one to help me. I've gotten myself out of plenty of scrapes throughout the years, but I can already tell this one is beyond my ample skills. Dark. Alone. Hungry. Based on the lack of output currently stinking up the front of my guy's shirt, I figure he hasn't eaten in at least a couple of days. Not only that, his mouth is practically glued shut from an absence of saliva. Add thirst to the growing list of things that indicate I'm up drak's creek without a paddle.

Broken, literally. Based on the pain, I can use that word properly and without any hint of exaggeration. I gently inspect his torso. Muted aches emanate from his back, and when I apply mild pressure to the area, the volume cranks up. I jerk my hand away. When I was fourteen and stole that Toyota Ring Jumper T15 and had my first off-planet joy ride, the guys from the ring of chop shops I worked for taught me a lesson about bringing unwanted attention on the gang. I had walked away from wrecking the T15 without any injuries. But my mentors broke a couple of my ribs and drove the point home by breaking my left hand.

And people wonder why I like to stay footloose and fancy free.
Letting people in your life always gets you hurt one way or another.
But I digress.

No doc needs to assess these ribs; they're broken for sure. But it's the leg I'm worried about. I know it's fractured. The crazy pain exhibited earlier is all the diagnostic info I need. The question is how badly? Palpating the area to find out means moving, which is not high on the good idea list. Unfortunately for me, bad ideas usually serve more as a challenge than a deterrent, and I'm naturally overrun with curiosity. *Mind over matter, Smullian my boy. Go to your happy place and the pain won't find you there.*

My happy place is the Jalpur Way Station. An entrepreneurial genius built it in the middle of seven different interstellar trading routes. People and aliens from all over the known universe pass through there at some point. Drinks are cheap, and so are the women. Marks arrive in droves, so the cash flows like water. I try to bring up the image of my favorite Jalpur bar, but it doesn't materialize. Instead, I find myself in Lydia's living room with its cheery curtains and thrift store couch. She's there too, sitting beside me.

I try to focus on the blue of her eyes while my fingers gingerly make their way toward my host's shin. The gentle prodding sends off some more fireworks, and I scream in response. The exhalation of air, of course, riles up the ribs again, and I sit panting weakly waiting for it all to be over. I take my mind back to the living room and try to picture Lydia again. She quickly jumps into focus, a pleasant smile on her face.

"I'm up the creek without a paddle," I tell her in my mind.

"You can do this, Smullian. You've been in tough scrapes before."

"Not like this."

"They've all prepared you for this moment. You can do it."

I steel myself and go back to the leg. Low on the shin, a fever burns. My host has an infection brewing along with a nasty break. Inspecting further down I hit an obstacle, his ankle bone jutting out of the skin. The pain reaches an ethereal level, and I float away.

I lean back and prop my feet on the ottoman. Lydia leans against me. Her hair smells clean, like a spring day. It's not too flowery or pungently sweet. Simple, clean like her. Her body seems to melt perfectly into mine. She fits. There's no awkward angles, just two separated pieces gliding together.

"*Dance Nation*?" she offers.

"Or you could give me a nice dental drilling. It'd be less painful."

"It's art. It's beautiful."

"It's reality television, the lowest form of 'art.'"

"Sure, it is. What do you call UFC?"

"Trained athletes meeting on the field of battle."

"You just described *Dance Nation*," she says, playfully slapping my chest. She settles against me again. "*Dead Company*?"

"Definitely, *Dead Co.*"

Ugh. She's domesticated me. It's so terrifying, so repulsive, so— wonderful. 'Me' of olden days wouldn't have understood the pure bliss of this connection. How could he? He never connected with anyone—a brace against heartache, against defeat, against living. But he was wrong. Because connection is far more pleasurable than anything he's experienced in his miserable life.

I come to and, at first, I'm confused. *Where did Lydia go?* Then reality fades in, and I remember I'm in hell or some Serbian prison. No, not Serbia, it's too hot and muggy. South American prison? I have no idea how long I've been out. The room is brighter now—sunlight filters in from somewhere. I look around. *Good news, I'm not down a well.* I see joists and beams as well as drywall. I look up, and there is no ceiling. Beams indicate where the floor should be. Above that is another floor. Dim sunlight pushes through the unfinished portion. *A building under construction? Where are the workers?*

I risk moving my head and look around me on the floor. To my right is a white candle burned low, wax puddled around it on the floor. Next to it rests a sketchbook and a pencil. On the left resides two Gatorade bottles, one with blue liquid in the bottom third and the other filled with a yellow liquid that definitely isn't Gatorade. The truth hits me hard. This is not South America. I'm much closer to the one place I'm starting to consider home.

"No!" I hurl into the emptiness. "He deserves better than this."

I've been in some pretty awful places, but this one is the worst. It might even be hell. As far as I can tell, there is no way out. Abandoned places usually have insects and rats, but I don't see any. Wherever this is must be pretty well boarded-up. On a positive note, the light from above casts all the cheer of an overcast day, and the rancid odor of vomit mixed with excrement perfumes the room. No one should die here.

"This is the closest thing you'll have to a tombstone," I mutter, picking up the sketch pad. The owner had written precisely on the back cover:

Property of David Hawthorne
Father to the fatherless, defender of widows—
—this is God, whose dwelling is holy.
Psalm 68:5

ll

know that Lydia and, probably, David would say that their god, this Father to the Fatherless, hadn't abandoned them, but was in fact helping them, and that's why I'm here. But if that's really the case then it just goes to show that their god may be "all-powerful," but he is, I hate to say, a moron. All-knowing doesn't describe someone who sends *me* as a white knight. If he's real, what is he thinking? I've never helped anyone in my life. I'm sure not *good*. There is nothing that qualifies me as the hero, but this god is using me to play the role. It's not smart and may be a little nuts. There are much better choices right here, right now in this century, in this city. I know because they've hosted me. Any of them, including Buttoned-down Marvin, are better choices for this little operation.

I'm already doing the only useful thing I can do for David. As much as I hate to say it, it benefits him that I'm here. He's in a subconscious state. The pain, the hunger, the thirst are all vague sensations to him right now. Today, he has a modicum of relief. But what about tomorrow when I'm gone? I don't know a lot about Christian philosophy, but I'm pretty sure hell is supposed to come after you die. David is living it. Some almighty Savior up there. If this is how he treats his followers, I sure as neth don't want to be one of them.

I sit and fume for a while at the injustice of it all. Lydia and David being so faithful…yet here they are stuck in this horrifying situation. David's basically on his deathbed, accompanied only by pain, writing out scriptures to the god that let this happen.

I pick up the sketchpad again, flipping it open. An exquisite drawing of a beetle adorns the first page…then a weathered pier over the river…an old man on a bench follows. I examine the picture closer and realize it's the gentleman we spoke to at the park. David's added so much detail the illustration could be a photograph. There are many more. Drawings from the park, the library, his home, even a couple from the school. Glancing through the book helps me take my mind off the intense thirst and hunger I am feeling. I resist the Gatorade, although his body is a vast desert devoid of any nutrients. There isn't much of the precious blue liquid left. David has been carefully rationing it, and I don't want to waste his efforts. I can wait a little longer.

My eyelids shutter closed. I force them open again. Add tiredness to the long list of maladies. No, not tiredness—ran a marathon in a 110 degrees level of exhaustion. I'd love to lean my head back and slide into dreamland, but I need to see if I can find any scrap of info about what landed David in this flarpdek.

About halfway through the book, the art changes. It's rougher than the earlier sketches, shakier. He must have started drawing these after he was stuck here. The lighting stinks, low sun during the day/candles at night. And pain accompanies his every move. It must be hard to hold the pencil steady. Even so, the art evokes more emotion that the earlier ones. Those were more detached observations of life. These pulse with passion, longing, and fear. I can feel it from the page: the fear that he will never leave this place, and the fear that he will never see the faces he's drawing ever again.

First is Lydia. He's drawn her in happier times: a wide smile, compassionate eyes. It's the way he wants to remember her. I can feel him saying goodbye with each stroke. Next is Madds. Hers emits a different vibe. He is mourning the loss of what could have been. Through his eyes, her radiance shines through. Her features are all drawn correctly and, yet, he has somehow elevated her plain proportions to beauty. He depicts her from a distance, a rare unobtainable thing. *Poor girl. She will never know what could have been.* The next few pages are drawings of his parents, Jesse. Some teens I don't recognize, but I bet are his friends in Nashville.

After all these portraits, I turn to what appears to be a comic book. Bronwen pops up in the first frame. I skim the page and recognize the work for what it is—an epitaph.

I stifle a laugh, and it comes out as more of a cough. "Leave it to David to write his last will and testament as a graphic novel," I mutter, returning to peruse the comic in detail. Bronwen approaches him while he's drawing at the park. *He did run into that lying, low life witch.*

"Excuse me, young man. I don't mean to bother you, but the spirits are speaking to me about you. They say you bear a great weight."

"Way to dial it in, Bronwen," I chide. "What teen doesn't think they're under a weight?" David was hooked though. His drawing depicts the interested upturn in his eyes.

"Ah, I see they are right. A heavy burden is upon you. A family member, is it?"

"Come on, Davey. She's fishing. Can't you see?" I wheeze into the empty room because I'm not capable of a shout. But of course, he couldn't see. His slumped shoulders and furrowed brows only made her bolder, more certain.

"A loss?" She put her hand on his arm. That tart dared touch him! "A parent—a sibling…"

"Both," David answers.

Don't talk to her, Davey. Once you talk to her, she has you hook, line and sinker.

"Both. Oh, you poor child. I see it now. An accident. So sudden."

"Of course, it was an accident. He's too young to lose them all naturally. She's not even that good," I add, like I can somehow warn him, but she has David snared now. His full attention is on her.

"The spirits are speaking loudly—I hear one voice above the others—it's female."

"Mom?"

"Yes, your mother." David didn't even realize he was feeding her the answers. He thought she really knew. That hag. After I'm sure David is fine, she's my number one mission.

"She wants you to know—speak up I can't hear you…" David drew Bronwen cocking her head. "Wait, don't go…" She paused then outstretched her hands in a meditative position and chanted. Finally, she spoke, "I'm so sorry, young man. The spirits have departed. They are such mercurial creatures."

"But, wait—what was Mom saying?"

"I know not, child."

"I have to know."

"Perhaps luck will favor us, and the spirits will return again in a fortnight or two."

"A fortnight? That's like two weeks, right?"

"You are correct."

"I can't wait two weeks."

Just like a drug; you're hooked from the first hit. I sigh.

"If they favor us that quickly. Often they wait quite a while."

"Come on. I need to know. Can't you try again?"

"Well, I want to help." Davey draws her eyes dripping with sympathy, her ring-laden hand pressed to her chest. "There is something I can do, but it is draining. It depletes my resources—emotionally and physically. So, you understand that it is a service I cannot provide for free. I do not enjoy speaking of money, but it is necessary. As you are young, I can meet your needs for a mere $500."

"Just like a dealer; the first taste is free, but after that you pay—big." I would have seen this for what it was. In fact, someone tried it on me once when I wasn't much older than my naive, guileless host. She suffered for it, as will Badapple Bronwen. But I digress.

Back to our regularly scheduled program, "Davey Gets Trapped in a Pit." *Isn't it supposed to be Daniel? Where are the lions?* I giggle, irritating my ribs. Someone needs to laugh at my jokes. Gray fog creeps into my vision, and I shake my head to keep awake. No air circulates in this room, and the midday heat creates a nice sauna. I'm slick with sweat. The sketchpad sticks to my fingers. I wrestle my attention back to the narrative.

"I don't have that much," Davey said. Bronwen started to disengage. "I can get about $350."

"Seeing as how you are so in need, I will accept that amount," she said, smiling. Here's the only time David's drawing has departed from reality, or at least I think it has, I can't entirely trust my mind. In the picture, her smile reveals fangs, dripping venom.

In the next frame, time jumped. Davey and Bronwen exchanged money in a room similar to this one.

"Are you sure it's okay for us to be here?" He asked, looking at the gaping hole left by the half-finished floor. I glance up through the missing ceiling to the third floor. *They must have met up there.*

"Of course. I've met others here many times. Spirits congregate in quiet places. Position the white candles at the points of the pentagram," she motioned to the far corner of the room. Davey drew himself unbuckling his backpack, then turning to Biddy Bronwen to ask a question. She was one step from the door.

"Hey, where are you going?" he asked.

She just glanced over her shoulder and sneered, then continued toward the door. Davey dashed toward her, closing the distance before she could clear the threshold. She turned, rushing back into the room, and pushed him hard on the chest with both hands. He stumbled backward and fell through the open floor, landing flat footed two stories down. His ankle snapped, throwing him back onto a pile of boards, and thus ended the ribs.

He drew her leaning over the hole, staring down at him broken on the dusty floor. The last frame is the same view, but she was gone. I flip through the pages, but there's no more. I figure he crawled to this door while the adrenaline gave him the strength. Only he found it sealed shut.

"That cancerous toad just left him there. She didn't mean to push him into the pit. That was an accident. Initially, running might have been panic, fear…but leaving him…for days, when she knew…she knew people were looking…that's just…that's just…" The gray fog returns, filling my vision. This time, I can't shake it, and sleep takes me.

III

"They're all just marks. You gotta stop thinking about them like they're people," Sharila said, taking a long drag on her cigarette, picking up on our earlier conversation as if the stop for sex was just a commercial break. She rose out of bed, the moon's light shining on her the curves of her body. It was hard to focus. At seventeen, I was already raring to go again and she did look delicious, but she was in the mood for a different kind of lesson. "Smulls, you and I are stronger, smarter, superior to them. We're on a different level. Does a lion feel guilty for eating the gazelle? Of course not, the gazelle's purpose is to feed him. We're lions, mighty predators. It's our nature to capture prey as much as it is theirs to be captured." She came back to the bed and leaned in front of me, her elbows braced, one hand over the other, cigarette dangling. "And what gazelles do the lions eat? The quick, healthy ones? No. They eat the slow, old, sick ones." She took a drag and blew it out slowly, her tongue darting out quickly and licking at the end. "Can they catch the young ones? Undoubtedly. But why bother when something just as tasty is within reach? The lions don't want to expend any more energy than they have to, and neither should you, Smulls. All your stupid rules only accomplish making you work harder and keeping you hungrier."

I nodded in agreement. I wasn't, of course, but I had to endure the lecture so that I could enjoy what comes after. It made Sharila happy to think she was my teacher. What she taught me when she was done philosophizing was all the sweeter when she thought I'd learned. A few more days, and I think I'll be done with her. She taught me more about cold reading and human nature in two weeks than I'd learned in all my seventeen years. Being with her would elevate me from a great grifter to an exceptional one. A legend for the ages, which is why I'd been with her this long. If I'm still learning, it makes sense to hang. Beyond the art of the con, she taught me more in the bedroom than I'd imagined possible. So, it was worth it to stay with her for the time being, even though I thought what she did was repulsive. I watched and learned, but I didn't actively participate in the bilking of the downtrodden. She thought she was grooming me so we could become a team. Her the psychic and me the shill, bringing in the customers. I didn't tell her it wasn't happening. I'm not a fool. The sex was too good.

"You understand what I'm saying Smulls?"

"Yeah. The lions take down the gazelles; it's the natural order."

"Good boy." She kissed me. Her lips tasted of nicotine, but I didn't mind. She slid into sheets and began a whole new lesson.

I wake up thirsty, confused. Then the pain and dankness remind me of where I am. I peel my tongue off the roof of my mouth and fruitlessly lick my lips. There's no liquid there to quench them. I take a sip of the Gatorade. Its sweet refreshment hits my mouth and, before I know it, I drag down three big gulps. *Nose to the grindstone, Smullian my boy. You need to save it for later. Tomorrow David will still need it.*

Sharila. I haven't thought about her and her Rolandi eyes in forever. When I met her, I'd been Earthside for a couple of days, living off the I'm-lost-and-can't-find-my-Mommy scam while I got the lay of the land. My perpetual babyface softened my seventeen years to a younger age, making the matronly-types trip over themselves to help me and feed me. In this case, that food was pilfren. I doubt it was actually pilfren. Those birds are non-indigenous, and my rescuer bought it for a song. However fried meat on a stick is delicious, even if its origins are dubious. But I digress.

There at Pike's Bazaar, fattening myself with ill-gotten gain, was where I first spied Sharila. She didn't need all the theatrics Badapple Bronwen incorporates. Her Rolandi ancestry did the job for her. Due to its influence, she was slightly duskier, slightly taller, and much more exotic than the average human woman. Her clear, green eyes closed the deal though. They weren't freakishly big, but large enough to imply she saw more than the visible spectrum. She exuded mystery, drawing in the marks before breathing a single word.

And "breathed" is the correct verb. She spoke softly, forcing the onlookers to crowd closer in order to hear her.

"Smart," I thought. "The quiet lures them in, makes them think what she's saying is mega important." I cleaned the last of the pilfren off the stick and threw it on the ground, edging nearer to see what else I could learn. I watched her cold read a few, effortlessly guiding them into expensive personal sessions. I immediately admired her craft, as well as her rack. But then she turned those eternal, fountain eyes on me. I slid into them.

"And you, young man. What are you seeking?"

I blinked and turned my head away from her gaze, which for her was like throwing chum in the water.

"I see it is painful," she whispered, reaching out and holding my hand. Physical touch, a grifter's method of creating a false sense of connection. I knew it but was still too young to control my reactions. I swallowed and pulled my hand away from hers. Memories of my mom's hand falling from mine in the hospital sprang to mind and tears formed in my eyes.

"You've lost someone close," she drove the knife in farther. Her brow furrowed in mock concern. Tears dribbled onto my cheeks. I dug deep to stanch the flow. *This charlatan doesn't get to talk about Mom and me like we matter. We're just a meal ticket to her.* I grabbed her hand and pulled her close.

"Stop now, or I'll spill all your secrets to this crowd. You'll lose today's payday and maybe get ruined in this bazaar forever." I hissed through clenched teeth.

Surprise flared in her eyes, but she quickly regained control, flashing a smile at the crowd. "This boy desires private counsel. Come back after lunch for more free consultations." Then she led me by the hand into the private section of her booth.

"Color me intrigued. What secrets were you planning on spilling?" she asked with a smirk.

I wanted to smack that smirk off her face but chose to do it verbally instead. "You talk quietly to make them come close. Plus, it makes them think they're in some secret club. You ask general questions and then watch the body language to see what direction to go. Darting eyes, swallows, crossed arms all mean there's something juicy there. That woman having trouble with her husband…you got that from the way she stuck him way at the end of the sentence. 'I'm on vacation with my husband' not 'Hubby and I are on vacation.' I could go on."

"No need. You know a lot about grifting for a kid."

"I'm not a kid."

"Oh yeah, how old are you?"

"Seventeen."

That's when her smirk changed to a smile. Her large, light green eyes drifted over my body, and I liked it. "Why, you're considered an adult in most regions."

"Yes, I am." *Maybe I can get something out of this.*

"Want to stay for lunch? I do readings for the Strosky booth up the aisle, and the owner gives me free food."

Angry or not, free food was free food. "Sounds good. No carran though. It tastes like rotten seaweed."

She gave a slight chuckle. "It does take a refined palate. You probably haven't had it served properly. I could order some bordon for you. It brings out the carron's nutty flavor." *What is she—a food critic? No, wait…she's trying to teach me. I can definitely get something out of this. I'll play along and feed her ego. See where this goes.*

When I did leave her asleep back on Earth. I never looked back. She'd served her purpose. I'd gleaned all I could and snatched all the cash. While the lingering thoughts of her kisses come back from time to time, she, her personhood, her identity do not. I never miss her or long for her. I needed her for a time, and then I took off.

I try shifting my position, but the motion sends crackles of pain down Davey's frame. I don't mind; it distracts me from the guilt crackling across my conscience. I can't exactly judge Bronwen for being cold. I felt Sharila deserved it. But Bronwen might figure David deserves it. I have my rules, and they make me feel superior to the likes of Shar and Broody Bronwen, but do they? Am I really different? I'm starting to think not so much. Maybe I'm a bad egg just like them—rotten to the core.

The light from outside is fading, but I resist lighting one of the candles. Like I was doing with the Gatorade, I need to preserve the meager stores. I read and reread the comic looking for any clues in the narrative or drawings as to where this pit is located, but there is nothing. How can I know so much, but not the one thing that really matters?

"You're going to screw it up." I peer into the darkness and see Benigno standing there. He's wearing a dark suit with a purple shirt and matching striped tie. "You've never helped anyone in your life but yourself. What makes you think you can get it right now? You're not capable of this."

Chuckles enters the scene and places a hand on Benigno's shoulder. "You got that right, Benny Boy. He's useless. David's doomed to die here in agony with no one to help him but this waste of humanity. The Father should have sent us. We actually know how to do a job and get it done."

Benigno squats down so that we're eye to eye. "You're a no-count nobody. People care about David and will be sorry when he's gone. Who's going to cry over you, Smullian? Nobody. You've drifted through life not making a difference to anyone or anything.

You'll be gone, rotting in the ground, and the universe won't even register the loss of mass."

Marvin enters, dressed in athletic clothes and one of those headbands. He's swinging a tennis racket like practicing for a serve. Swish, swish. He stops the swinging and looks me in the eye.

"They're right, you know. You destroy everything you touch. Look what you did to my car, my baby, my pride and joy. You can't help it. It's just the way you are. You like to think about Lydia, but what would you do if you really had her? One day with you, and she'd be ruined. You could convince her to be with you—you're a good talker—but what would you do to her? Methodically strip away everything about her that was peace and light. She'd become a cynical waste of breath like you. A poor reflection of all the things that were pure about her."

My dad wanders in, swigging from a bottle. "You'll destroy her, just like you did your mother. She was a looker before you. A body that was divine. Then you came along. You bloated her up and stretched her out. Looking at her made me want to gag. You did that. Chased me away. What man is going to want a woman with a snot-nosed brat in tow? Huge turn-off. Before you, she could have made decent money in the clubs, but not after you ruined her."

"No, she loved me," I say.

"Pbfht."

"She did. I was her favorite boy."

"Sure, Smullian. She loved having to lie and cheat just to keep you fed. She loved hustling drunks just to keep a roof over your head. You were a burden and a drain, plain and simple. In fact, she died just to be free of you."

"Don't say that!" I scream. The pain knocks me out of the illusion. I pant raggedly, trying to hold on until the pain ebbs again. "She loved me," I whimper. No one answers. The specters are gone for the moment.

The faint hope of light faded long ago, and the darkness is creeping me out. I don't know if that was a dream or if Davey's fevered brain produced me one doozy of a hallucination. Either way, it's time to light that candle. Giggles shudder through my midsection.

"Houston, I think we have a problem. Neil Armstrong appears to have a bum leg. We may have to scrap the mission." The giggles threaten to mature into full-on guffaws. I fight to keep them at bay with short breaths. The last thing I want is to expand his rib cage. Hot, stale air hangs in the room. It's Florida, after all, where sunset does not promise lower temperatures. As I fumble along the ground feeling for the lighter, even the concrete is warm.

My fingers land on it and, miracle of miracles, it sparks to life with one strike. The candle takes a little longer with its stubby wick, but soon I have the comfort of a weak, yellow, inconsistent flame. In the glow, I notice Madds' prediction of a smiley-faced lighter for the irony was correct. *I wonder if she'll ever click again with someone like she does with him.*

"Ugh, Smullian. You make me miss vomiting. This teenage brain soaked in dehydration and infection is making you more melodramatic than a South Korean soap opera," I chide myself. "Seriously, dude. You're five crackers shy of a loaf."

To focus my increasingly confused mind, I pick up the sketchpad again and hold it up to the dim light. As before, I find no clues to where we are. Makes sense. Davey figures whoever finds the pad knows the where; they'd be more interested in the who, why, and how. As I flip the pages, I notice a letter I hadn't seen earlier in the day.

Dear Lydia,

It's funny to me how many times we drove by these buildings and made up stories about the fairy creatures that lived here and their wars with the mole people. I hoped something magical would happen here and, instead, I got ripped off and trapped in this empty, sad place.

I knew what you'd have said about the seance. That's why I didn't tell you about it. But she knew things, Lydia. She knew. I know what the Bible says about it, but I listened to her anyway. I wanted to believe. Remember that verse in Proverbs that says to stay away from the strange woman. Yeah. No excuses from me. I knew better in lots of ways, but I wanted it to be true so badly. To talk to Mom and Dad and Jesse one more time, to apologize for being such a butt that day. To tell them I loved them. It seemed worth it. Clearly, I was wrong.

Remember how you say that God doesn't make bad things happen to us. It's the result of my poor choices or someone else's poor choices. Well, I guess me being here is a bit of both. I'm going to go with mostly hers though. Haha. She is the one who pushed me. She's the one who saw me down here and didn't send help. You know I spent the first several hours lying here thinking help would be there any moment. That she'd called, and they were on the way. When night fell and the darkness settled in, I realized no one was coming. I'm not sure anyone ever will. I keep hoping, though.

I've spent a lot of time here praying. And I want to ask you to forgive me. I haven't made things easy for you. I've been caught up in my stuff and haven't thought about how it must be for you. I've been a jerk. Worse. I was a thief. Most of that money was yours, and I just took it. Thought I deserved it. If I'd really believed Bronwen was on the level, I'd have brought you too. Didn't both of us have the right to talk to them? I think way down deep I knew it wasn't true, but I didn't want to listen to that voice.

I guess if I want you to forgive me, I have to forgive her. That's a lot harder. 'Cause I wanna say what she did is way worse. But sin is sin, right. Well, I'm still praying about that one. I hope you can forgive her too.

It would be easy to blame God. But it was his voice I was ignoring—the Bible, the Holy Spirit—telling me it wasn't on the level. You've kept telling me that God is with us in the storms; He doesn't take them away always. Well, I can feel him here. So even if help doesn't come, don't worry. I wasn't alone.

Love,

David

"He's praying to *forgive* her? That troll? I don't understand Lydia and him. They're certifiable." A picture of Sharila's green Bette Davis eyes flashes through my mind. Would I want her to forgive me? Before this week, I wouldn't have given it much thought. But yeah, I did her pretty dirty, intentionally. It wasn't an accident that spiraled out of control. Forgiveness would be nice.

A fresh wave of pain hits me, and I can't hold back the groan, which in turn riles up the injured ribs. There is no break from this agony. It's just pain and then stronger pain. Never does it ebb away for a moment of sweet relief. My mind travels, drifts into the fog. The sound of my own heavy breathing takes me back to the hospital room where my mother died. The last days she just slept and breathed. A slow, rhythmic inhalation and exhalation. The nurses had told me it was normal and meant she was in the last stages of life.

I would try to rouse her and get her to wake up and speak to me one more time. To say my name. To put her hand on my brow. To stroke my hair. I had this crazy fear that once she was gone, I'd disappear, vanish out of existence. Her knowledge of me meant I was someone. Her love somehow kept me grounded in this plane. What if I was her illusion, and when she was gone, I would go too? Every time she said my name, stroked my hair, held my hand she grounded me in this world. What would happen to me if she was gone? In and out she breathed, but never uttered another word.

I see her there in the dim light. The hospital bed with all its sensors and leads telling me her heart is still beating, but I know it won't much longer.

"Smully," she says weakly.

"Yes, Mom."

She holds out her hand to me, touches my cheek. "You're a real boy. You know it. You're a strong boy. I raised you to be one. You can do this. You can. I believe in you."

"What can I do? I'm powerless. I'm not even in control of my body. They have it out there tucked away in the future. There's nothing I can do. I can't jump out of David and go for help. I'm stuck here."

"You care for him. That is enough. You'll figure out the rest when the time comes."

"That sounds good, Mom, but —"

"No excuses, son. You can do this. I raised you. I know you. You're a survivor. Be one for David."

The fog creeps in again. I rub my eyes, trying to wake myself up. The sting of salt from my hands accomplishes the job nicely. I've got to stop sweating. I'm losing liquid, and I don't have any to replace it. I rub impatiently at my head. The innocent movement irritates my ribs, and I drop my arm still again. The pain is like an itch, compelling me to alleviate it. Sparking my muscles to move and find a position that doesn't have the pain. But there is no position and moving makes it all so much worse. I brace my arms on the floor and try a gentle shift of my hips because the pain isn't just in David's ankle and ribs. It's everywhere, screaming, groaning for attention, for relief—finding none. I wouldn't be surprised if David has pressure sores on his back and buttocks. He's been leaning on this door and sitting on this hard concrete for four days.

Who am I kidding? Even if by some miracle, and it would be a miracle for sure, someone finds him before he gives his last shattered gasp, he will have a long, painful recovery. An extended hospital stay for starters. Physical therapy for the leg. Surgery. Rounds of antibiotics for the infection. I know he said he wanted to live yesterday, but what about when he's back in his body tomorrow? Will he want to live then? I only need to look at his drawings to know the answer to that. He wants to live for Lydia and Maddie.

If it were me instead of him, what would I be holding out for? What spark would keep me going? Last week, it would be nothing. I had no people I cared to see again. No unattained goal to keep me hoping. This week though—this week I have David. That's some existential head scratching there. I want to stay alive for David while I'm inside David.

"The hope is in me! Hahahaa."

As long as we're doing stand-up, I want to stay alive for Lydia—a girl who doesn't know what I look like and has only had Cyrano-style conversations with me. She knows nothing of Smullian O'Toole. I mean nothing to her, yet I am drawn to her like a moth to flame. She is light in a dark world, and I want more of it. Like a plant stretching beyond the canopy for a few rays, I crave her smile. Her sweet face. I have got to make it through today, for David, for me. I can't help but feel that saving David will somehow save me. That this will be the thing that redeems me—pulls me up out of the pit of isolation I've dropped myself in and drags me out into the world.

"Dude, stop with the melodrama. This ain't a gothic romance. It's life, and life sucks for everyone. No one gets a break in life. Orphans are made and then more flarp happens to them. Nobody is getting saved here. Not David and sure as heck not me." I lean my head back and sigh. Hope is a dangerous drug. I learned that a long time ago. This day will end. Tomorrow will be just as fruitless, and David will die here. Alone in this dank, dark nowhere of a place. It's funny that David and Lydia dreamed this was a magical land with fairies and rainbows, but they were wrong. It's an oubliette. A place to be forgotten

"What a fantastic metaphor for life. You believe it will be beautiful but instead it's a pit in which you'll be forgotten. What a lie we tell ourselves. Here we are, David, you and me, the forgotten. Here we'll rot."

"Is David forgotten?" A man stands in the blackness, yet I can see him perfectly well. He is tall with silver and white hair. His pants and jacket are a matching silver gray. Underneath the jacket is a white shirt with a precisely knotted silver tie. His skin is pale, but not white, and it lightly shines as if dusted with luminescent silver. His nose was very straight and set above two thin, almost gray, lips. He stands with his fingers loosely laced in front of him, as if he were at a board meeting. He's not familiar to me, and I'm great with faces.

"Who are you?" I ask.

"Is David forgotten?"

I shake my head. "Not now, but he will be. Lydia will remember, of course. Maybe Madds will have a fond memory of first love. Burnsey might remember that kid, but once they're gone, no one will know him. No one will ever speak of him or think of him, yet his bones will still be here. Alone."

"I sustain him. I know his name. I am eternal."

"Sure. I must have drummed you up from Davey's brain."

"Are you forgotten?"

"Okay. I'll play along. No one remembers me. It's kind of the point. I slip in, do the con, and slip out. I'm a ghost. Heck, I'm a prisoner in the most sophisticated penal system in the world and even they have forgotten me. It's been four days, and they haven't figured out I'm missing. Out of the loop, as it were."

"I have never forgotten you. Even here in this place I am with you as I have always been."

"Yeah, you've always been with me. Where were you when my mother died?"

"I walk that corridor with you. You chose to leave."

"I chose to leave, and so my life sucking is my fault."

"Your choices determine your path. However, I walk it with you."

"Yeah, well, thanks for all you *did* for me."

The slightest upturn reaches corners of his lips. "No, son, it is not what I do for you. It is what I keep from befalling you."

Suddenly, my mind floods with images of all the near-misses I've had in my misspent youth. Times which would have been catastrophes but weren't. The sex trafficking ring, for one. The time I barely ditched those meathead bodyguards on Theta Outpost. Another where a partier died from bad jawa, but I didn't take enough for it to kill me. Made me sick enough to never use again though—I look up at the gray man.

"Still doesn't make any sense you sending a felon like me to help David."

His perfect teeth actually shine in the smile this time. "Smullian, child, I didn't send you to help David. David is helping you."

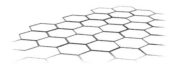

PART FIVE

GRUDGING ACCEPTANCE

The air reeks of alcohol and antiseptic. It triggers my daily retching.

"He's purging," someone yells.

Rough hands roll me to my side as I empty my stomach and what may still be lurking in my upper intestines. *I did it! They found Davey. Finally. I did something right.* The retching subsides, and the same hands right me.

"Ugh, that's a mess," someone remarks, a lower voice than before.

My eyes aren't working right. All I can see is brightness and shadows moving in my periphery. I try to lift my head and look around, but my neck muscles rebel at the motion. My heads flops back down.

"Hold tight, SO51399. You haven't fully integrated. Keep still."

"Wait," I try to say, but my vocal cords don't seem to be working either. I shake my head and try to sit up.

"Whoa, SO51399. I said to be still. You'll be fully integrated in a moment." *Integrated? Doesn't make sense. Why're they calling me that number? My name's David.*

"Heart rate is stabilizing." I hear someone say behind me. My eyes may not be able to see, but my ears are having no trouble. There are several people in this room, moving about, their clothes swishing like paper. I hear beeps and a distant intercom although I can't make out what it's proclaiming. I'm in a hospital, definitely, so I must still be David. *But why is that guy calling me SO51399? Did they find him as a John Doe? Why not call him that?* The light is blinding…it hurts. I close my eyes. It makes sense. David's been in near darkness for days.

I'm edgy. There's too much activity in the room, coming from directions I can't see. Faceless people are pushing me, attaching leads, saying things I don't understand. The sounds assault me. My eyes burn. I can't see. *What's happening to me?* My breath comes in rushed, ragged heaps. *I have to sit up.* Things will make sense if I can just sit up and look around. Orient myself. My exhalations and inhalations tumble on top of each other. Voices swirl in circles around me. My clothes shrink; my hands want to claw them free, but can't. *I need to sit up.* I force myself upright and hear a gasp. Hands are on me again, shoving me down.

"SO51399, be still. You are not fully integrated, and you could hurt yourself." Behind this female voice, I hear a male voice.

"I hate these emergency reintegrations. We don't have time to prep the body. They should have given us a few hours' warning."

"Orders are orders."

"Don't listen to me; I'm only a highly trained medical doctor, but you know better, government bean counter. Would a few hours have really made a difference in this inmate's case? A few hours so we can do this right."

Vomit bursts forth from my throat without any warning. I'm rolled on my side again. My heart pounds wildly.

"He's seizing," someone yells as my body takes on a life of its own. My back arches with such severity that I think it might snap. My hands and feet clutch into fists, and the rest of me waggles and jerks like a fish on a line. I feel a sharp stab in my upper arm, and everything fades. Just as the world goes dark, it hits me. He said *inmate*.

I come to again. The light still glares, but not painfully so. I can hear the drone of machines, but no people.

"Hello?" I call out weakly.

Squelchy footsteps approach from across the room. Icy fingers grasp my wrist, checking my pulse.

"How are you feeling, SO51399?"

"Thirsty."

"I'll get you some water. You threw up quite a bit earlier. I imagine your throat is burning."

It's not that. David's dehydration still inhabits me. The pain is gone, but I still feel the compulsion, the utter need for water. She slips a straw into my mouth, and I suck down the cool liquid. SO51399 is *my* ward number. Someone earlier called me *inmate*. *Is it possible I'm back in my own body?*

"When am I?

"You're back here in the good old twenty-fourth. I heard there was some kind of error in your programming. Don't worry, they'll get it all fixed up in a jiff. Meanwhile, I'll bet you're happy to be back in civilization, if only for a little while."

"No, I need to go back."

"Well, I don't know about any of that. Someone higher up will come in and talk to you about those logistics."

"You don't understand. I need to be put back in now," I urge, grabbing her arm.

She snaps it free. "If you want to go back, you need to behave yourself while you're here. Now drink all your water, like a good patient, or I'll have to have a say with your Life Modification treatment specialist."

"Bring her down here now. And the warden. It's a matter of life and death. I need to go back."

"You know policy. You cannot speak with anyone until you are cleared medically, which you are not. Sit back and relax or your heartbeat will never regulate." She about-faces with a sharpness that a Nazi would admire and marches off, warning me the conversation is over not just now, but permanently. She vanishes, and I'm left alone, trying to figure out what to do next. Except I can't, because they pumped me full of some pretty strong drugs. One moment I'm awake, the next—

When I come to, it's easier to orient to my surroundings. "I'm in a hospital." I mutter. "In the twenty-fourth." Pudgepot is back, tapping at the monitors.

"I see you're awake, SO51399." Cold hands hold my wrist, searching for a pulse. They teach an entire course called "Manual

Medical Techniques" in nursing schools. Despite all the future's advances, patient health declined over time. After extensive and expensive studies, researchers found that nothing beats the assurance of physical touch. *Except for hers! Does she plunge her hands in ice first?* Her fingers jump to my forehead. If I wasn't already awake, those frigid digits would bring me to life pretty quick. "Do you know where you are?"

"Hospital ward."

"Good. Do you know when you are?"

"Twenty-fourth century."

"Good." She says with the same tone of voice she might use praising a toddler for making poo in the potty. I'm trying to hold in the frustration. I need to know about Davey, but this woman doesn't have the imagination to help me. She can't see beyond her prescribed tasks. Probably why she's nursing in a prison instead of one of the bustling cutting-edge hospitals on a main planet. Pudgepot excels at following directions because she is not capable of original thought.

"Your levels are all within parameters. I'll notify the doctor. Hopefully, we'll have you out of here and back in a cell by the end of the day."

"How long?"

"I just told you 'end of the day.'" She's getting snippy again. I can't afford to have her on my bad side. I need to stay in her good graces.

"I'm sorry. I meant how long since reintegration?"

"I don't have that information. You've been in my care for four and a half hours, most of it asleep. Reintegration makes one quite tired." I figured that one out for myself. I feel like she's talking to a toddler again. "I don't know how long you were in the procedure room."

For David, this is an eternity. He doesn't have time for me to be out of commission. I don't have a second to waste around here. I need to get back to him—fast. But Pudgepot isn't going to help me. No point in needling her about it.

I lie back and piece back together all the weird fragments I've had since I came around the first time. Emergency Reintegration. The emergency must have been the discovery that my Life Mod has been off script for several days. Some tech found the glitch and reported it to some superiors, who reported back to the warden, who reported it to the board of governors, who gave the order to yank me out of Life Mod. Do not pass go, do not collect 200 dollars, do not take time to prep the body. That's what it would be to them: a faceless, nameless blob of flesh. Certainly not a person, certainly not someone worthy of a heads-up or proper reintegration.

Reintegration is different than biotransposition. In biotransposition, the host's body is warmed up, as it were. The brain has been functional and in control of limbs, systems, and organs. Brainhitching acts a little like switching drivers while the car is in motion. The vehicle may swerve and decelerate for a moment but moves back up to speed quickly. The pain and vomiting are that swerve and deceleration, for all intents and purposes.

Reintegration behaves like cranking up an old car on a cold day. If it starts at all, it will sputter a few times before turning over: the electrical may misfire, and it will be several long minutes before the heat is up and running. My body has been in suspended animation for 781 days. To guard against atrophy, robots have been giving my muscles electrical stimulation. My brain hasn't had a passenger, much less a driver. My gray matter has been sleeping in the back seat. Successful reintegration, as it was explained during my orientation, requires several hours of prep work. The body must be warmed up literally and figuratively before my consciousness can take over. With prep time, the process goes smoothly. Without it, well, there's vomiting, seizures, unresponsive systems, and confusion. Lots and lots of confusion.

So, they've reintegrated me. What now? What's the plan? I could waste time pondering it, but I'm not going to know anything until I talk to my Life Modification treatment specialist. That's a corrections counselor, in your parlance. And I can't do that until I'm medically cleared. I resist the urge to call back Pudgepot and ask how it's going with the doc, because she's the type to drag her feet with an annoying patient.

And that leaves me no other choice than to wait. I hate waiting. I need to be moving, taking action, not sitting around contemplating my navel while Davey rots in the past. My future, my destiny. Davey's future, er past, er future-past—*I wonder how Burnsey would conjugate these verbs? What tense would be proper here?* But I digress.

All of this is out of my control. I'm in my own body, but I'm still impotent and powerless. Replay the theme of the week. I've gone from footloose and fancy-free, got no strings on me to the Father's puppet. I haven't felt this way since I was twelve years old, and I promised myself then I would never feel this way again. Even when I got pinched, I got into Life Mod—the cushiest bid out there. As far as I was concerned, Life Mod was just a bump in the road to getting me back to the life I wanted.

I think about the gray man. He would say this easy time was his doing, holding back the bad stuff. But that was just a hallucination. *Then why did it feel so solid?*

I inhale, fill my cheeks, and exhale a cleansing breath of air. Just like Burnsey. I chuckle. These people have worked their way under my skin for sure. I'd laugh more if it weren't so terribly tragic.

I know how the next few days or possibly even weeks are going play out. According to *Acceptable Conduct and Behavior for Life Modification Therapy Candidates,* "In the unlikely event that an error in the programming of the Life Modification Therapy System precipitates the necessity of an emergency reintegration, a full and thorough investigation of the candidate and audit of the databases and system will be performed under close supervision of the board of governors according to procedures laid out in Subsection VIII of the Life Modification Therapy Code Enforcement and Processes Manual." Something went way wrong with the system, and The Powers-That-Be are going to want answers. The techies will be spending every waking hour going back through the code looking for spurious 1s and 0s, auditing the databases, and examining the Candidate Selection System with a magnifying glass.

Everyone else, managers, supervisors, coordinating supervisors, interns, secretaries, and their next-door neighbors will be looking at me to see if I had a part. There will be lots and lots of interrogations. They'll ask questions, plug me into various diodes and electrical doo dads, ask more questions, run neuro scans, ask the same questions in a different way. Then I'll finally have the opportunity to talk with my Life Modification treatment specialist who will decide, in the end, whether or not to let me continue in Life Mod. If they do put me back into the system, is there any guarantee that they will put me back in the same time and place? Doubtful, but I suppose there's a chance. It's the only thing I can hope for.

Goal 1: Get back in Life Mod, which means I better get my story straight. How much do I tell them? Enough to prove my innocence, but not so much they diagnose me with Biotransposition Psychosis, aka Ripper Madness. No need to bring up disembodied voices.

At least, now I have something to do. It's a fact of neurolinguistics that if you practice a story long enough it stops being a fabrication and embeds in your long-term memory. It comes across to investigators, eye pattern readers, and neural polygraphs like the truth. That's why the fuzz ask the same questions over and over, they're trying to trip the perp up, catch him in an inconsistency. It works on lesser criminals, but not Smullian O'Toole. I can make the most preposterous fable read like documented history.

A task helps me. Because I was wrong about goal one. Goal 1 Amended: Get cleared medically. None of the relentless investigation starts until Doc says I'm healthy enough. Doc won't clear me until my vitals are all hunky dory. This stress bounces my numbers all over the place. I can hear the annoying beeps of the machine I'm attached to and know it's outside of healthy parameters. I close my eyes and, in my mind, travel back to the moment I was woken by Marvin's alarm clock. Somewhere in the background I hear the machine's high-pitched beeps slow to a rhythmic pace as I craft the story of a poor Life Mod inmate trapped in a situation beyond his control. I smile. It's like being back in the game. If I do this right, they may feel so bad for me they reduce my time. Goal 2: Get back in Life Mod. Goal 3: Get a shorter bid.

I spend the next several hours running my story in my head. I try to anticipate every twist and convolution they may try to throw at me. I'm thoroughly satisfied, but one reason I am the best is I never rest until the job is done. Do the job right, and there's plenty of time and loot for recreation after. So, I run it again and again.

Doc walks in. He a schlubby sort of man; in fact, he's like an old hound dog in human form. Long face, slumped shoulders, wrinkled clothes. The staff in this place are definitely the cream of the crop.

"How are you feeling, Mr. O'Toole?" he asks, looking me right in the eyes. That's when I see it, concern and a spark of intelligence. *He called me by my name, not my ward number. He'd have had to look that up before he came in.* Before this whole screw-up, my natural instinct would have been hostile, regardless of what I read in this man's eyes. I'd have chalked it up to a profession that requires a look of compassion, that it was just a well-practiced tool of the trade, no different than the hours he spent practicing suturing. But now—I trust him. *Ridiculous. The last few days have certainly scrambled my eggs*

"Fine. I ain't gonna lie; I was woozy earlier, but I'm rarin' to go now." It's my *aww shucks* persona. Charming, a little slow, harmless. I break it out when I need to play an authority figure. They feel superior, and thus more likely to bestow a blessing on this poor little underling. No one in the legal system knows Smullian O'Toole at all. They've only met aww shucks guy.

"I imagine you were," he says, chuckling. Hook set. "Your blood pressure and heartbeat look fine. But you did suffer a seizure during reintegration. I'd feel better if we ran another neural scan. I can schedule that for tomorrow."

Tomorrow! Nooo! I need to get this show on the road. Calm down. Nose to the Grindstone, Smullian. It's never mattered more in your miserable life.

"Whatever you say, Doc. But I really feel finer than Lortrel wine. Are you sure that's necessary? I've only got two hundred days left, and I want to get back to my girl. She's got the prettiest eyes you've ever seen."

The doc pulls a chair over and sits next to the bed. Another considerate move. He's putting himself on my level instead of towering over me.

"I understand your impatience. I do. I couldn't imagine being separated from my Mary for that long, but you want to go back to her whole and functional, don't you? If we rush things now, there could be complications. I'm not promising anything, but maybe I could move the Board to allow her to visit while you're out. I could tell them it would aid in your recovery."

Why is he so nice?

"Gee thanks, Doc. But it wouldn't work; she's too far away… (three hundred years away)… and she's gotta watch our little boy Davey. I don't see how she could make it. You thinkin' about it sure means a heap."

"If you change your mind, let me know. I'd be happy to facilitate it. But in regard to you, I do think it's best to observe you overnight and run a scan in the morning." He pats my arm; he actually pats my arm, like with affection. Why couldn't I have gotten the old codger I assumed he was? I can't even be mad about this turn of events. He is doing what he thinks is best for me. When he stands, his lab coat shifts, and a small cross pin on his shirt pocket reflects the bright lights of the room.

"You really believe that?" I ask.

"What?"

I point to the pin.

"Yes, I do."

"How? I mean you're a smart guy."

"You mean how can a man of science believe in all this superstitious hoodoo?" he asks with a mischievous grin.

"Well, yeah."

"I have never found the two mutually exclusive. There is truth in science, but there is more truth in my faith. I'd love to talk with you about it more, but I am forbidden by my contract with the board. If you are truly interested in Christianity, there's a religion port in the prison library. You can speak with an approved, licensed professional there. It is your right, as a prisoner, to pursue the religion/belief system of your choice. When I discharge you tomorrow, you should ask to go. Once requested, it must be honored. Sleep well tonight, Mr. O'Toole."

"Uh, Doc, do you think you could ask your, uh, Friend, to help some people I know? They know him, and they could really use it."

"I will," he says. "But why don't you ask him yourself?"

"Pssht," I say. "Why would he listen to a felon like me?"

He cocks his head, those hound dog jowls wobbling. "My friend doesn't care what you've done. Those things don't matter to him. See you tomorrow, Mr. O'Toole." He turns and leaves the room.

"Thanks, Doc." I say to the empty air. *He would do well in my field.* He has a countenance that belies his intelligence.

People wouldn't expect that old hound-doggy face to be capable of deceit or craftiness. I enjoyed the way he flawlessly found a way to introduce his faith regardless of the handcuffs the regulations placed on him. I wonder how many other inmates he's reminded of their right to religion and how to find it inside these walls. Long ago, The Powers-That-Be stopped priests, shamans, and holy men from visiting prisons, but legally they still had to provide a modus for prisoners to worship. Thus, the religion port was invented. Press the appropriate button and an inmate has access to the clergy of their choice for five-minute intervals.

I'll take Doc's advice and visit the port. I'd never spill about the Father to the Fatherless to the screws that run Life Mod, but I can't deny that he's at the bottom of this little glitch. I guess it's time to find out more about him. Know what I'm dealing with. Financial Planning Lesson Three—Thoroughly vet all business associates or find out everything you can about the unknown deity currently meddling in your life.

"How far the mighty have fallen. I can't believe the great Smullian O'Toole is even considering religion. God! Pssht." I mutter, but then catch myself. *You have to be on your best behavior. Pudgepot could be listening. Can't have her catch you talking to yourself. She'd love to report that to her higher-ups.*

I admit my mind is in a different place than it was four days ago. Whether I believe or not, all the people I've connected with in the past few days have believed in this hoodoo, to quote the doc. Even the doc! What are the chances that I land the one Christian doctor in the entire prison system? More than that, I can't deny the effect on their lives. It's certainly something to ponder. But not now. I need to go over my story again. It has to be flawless before *They* throw me in the hot seat.

II

I've waited six grinding, mind-numbing, torturous days to speak with my Life Modification treatment specialist, and now I'm waiting again. She's late. Why? I don't know. I think it's in the job description: Be late by forty minutes to every appointment. I've told my story so many times in the last few days I've started reciting it in my sleep, but the good news is I'm pretty sure I've achieved goal 3. While they're trying to decipher me, I've been cold reading them. And one thing is for sure, they're stumped. Grade A stupefied as to what's happened with their precious, unhackable, indestructible Life Mod. They're also pretty sure I'm just some poor ward that got caught in this grand cluster bomb and are starting to worry I might consider legal action against their precious system.

That's when the bribes like a shorter sentence will begin. I need to decide how much I'll let them grovel. It's a fine line between getting as much as you can and getting greedy. Greediness leads to losing everything. Many a con has lost a good payday reaching for a great one. I learned early on that a mayor's wallet in the pocket is better than a senator's briefcase on the curb. I almost lost my right hand groping for that one. But I digress.

I don't want to push it too far. I need them to put me back in Life Mod for Davey's sake. A shortened sentence would be nice, but I don't need a pardon at this point or, worse, some guilt-ridden hush money and a ride out of this sector of the galaxy. No, this interview will be the most important of the week.

My Life Modification Treatment Specialist rushes in. Her tan skirt has a small dark stain indicating she ate in transit, and her dark hair, which probably lay smoothly across her brow this morning, sticks out errantly. Even her rich, chocolate skin somehow manages to look sallow. She checks her holopad and smiles.

"So, Mr. O'Toole." I met her a couple of times before I went into Life Mod. She cares as much as she is able. I imagine once she dreamed of helping change the system, of rehabilitating felons. But then she graduated, and a couple vampires named red tape and crushing caseload almost drained her bleeding heart. She still has enough red cells left to try her anemic best. Hence, checking the holopad for my name.

"I've been briefed on the case, of course," she says, crossing her arms on the table and fixing her flat brown eyes on mine. "So, I'm not going to make you run through the whole thing again. I'm sure you're tired of talking about it."

Did I mention she loves aww shucks guy? "You can say that twice," I answer with a light chuckle.

"I'm just going to ask your feelings about a couple of particular instances. Is that alright with you?"

"I'm fine with whatever it'll take to get this ball rolling."

"I understand. I imagine it's been frustrating."

"I get it. I do. People want to know what jelly jammed up the gears. I just want to get on with my sentence, you know."

"What a positive attitude, Mr. O'Toole." She jots a note on the holopad. "At one point a police detective hosted you, correct?"

"Yes."

"What was that experience like for you?"

"Scary."

"Scary in what way?"

"First of all, I didn't think us Life Mod felons were supposed to, you know, be cops. I thought there was a rule or somethin'. So, I thought maybe should call in sick, but there's is also a rule about that. Either way I might be breakin' a Life Mod rule. I didn't know what to do. I don't want to get in trouble." I pause for effect. *Goal 3.* "I decided it was better to do the job. But then there was the job! I'm not that kind of felon. I do petty scams. I'm not muscle; I don't do hold-ups. What if somethin' went down? I wouldn't know what to do."

"You carried a weapon."

"That was part of the problem! As I said, I'm a scammer. I don't know nuthin' about guns. The whole day was freaky. I just tried to keep my head down and do the job. I did solve a crime, though."

"How did that feel?"

"Pretty good. I guess it helps to be a cop if you know how criminals think." I chuckle. *Time to slide in Davey. Goal 2.* "I also started this other case. We thought it was a runaway. A fifteen-year-old boy. Kind of reminded me of me. His parents had passed."

"An orphan like you were?"

"Yeah."

"Empathy. Pride in a job well done. You've made some big strides. We'll talk more about the boy in a minute. I know he comes up again. Let's talk about the teacher. There's a strict rule about minors—"

"I know! It was like the cop thing. What rule do I break? Either way I could get more time in Life Mod. Either way I'm screwed." Another pause. *Poor little ward stuck in Life Mod gone mad. Let's give him a shorter sentence, shall we?* "I made the same decision. Do the job. This time I made sure I was never alone with a minor. I figured it was the best solution. What else could I do?"

"Mr. O'Toole, I believe you behaved admirably in a difficult situation."

"Pssht. I was just trying to hang in there until Life Mod figured out what was happenin'. I'm sure someone else would've handled it better."

"I am not sure there was a better or a right way in this scenario. It has never happened before." She glances back at her holopad. "Did you enjoy teaching?"

"I ain't gonna lie, sometimes those little twerps make you wanna snatch em up by their ears. I didn't though. But other times when they paid attention and got it, that was cool, like, hey, they're excited 'cause of somethin' I said."

"Excellent. I believe we might be able to point you to some satisfying work when your sentence is complete. Not education, mind you, but something," She sets down the pad and focuses her eyes on mine again. "Now the boy."

"David."

"Right. David. According to your story and our data, he'd suffered some serious injury."

"Yes."

"I'm sorry you had to undergo such cruel and unusual punishment. You know that's n—"

"I didn't mind."

"Excuse me?"

"I didn't mind. I don't get off on pain; don't get me wrong. He didn't have to feel it that day you know. Davey, he's just a kid. He got a break for a little while. I didn't mind."

"This came up earlier in our conversation. You seem to have formed a connection with him."

"Seemed like it was all about him," I chuckle trying to play it light. I have to play it careful here. There's a fine line between declared rehabilitated and diagnosed with Ripper Madness.

"In what way?"

"Everyone I hitched knew him somehow. The accountant on the first day helped him and the sis with taxes. It was his car that was stolen and ended me up at the cop shop where I heard David was missing in the first place." *Wait…I had to be in the cop shop… The Father wanted me in the cop shop…But I was there because the Ferrari was stolen…What if I had driven the Volvo? Would the whole plan have fallen apart? Or…did it matter what car I drove?*

"Mr. O'Toole?"

"Oh, sorry. I was lost in the salt as the ol' timers say on Galwa. Anyway, everything seemed to point to im, you know."

"I understand. All of us from the board on down are searching for some meaning in all of this. You, especially, have been through a traumatic event." I think she truly sympathizes, but at the same time her tone is dismissive. "You'd want to find a purpose in it. But you shouldn't make connections that are not there."

I can think of a connection I'd like to make with your face right now, but it would adversely affect Goals 2 and 3. "That sure makes a lot of sense. Things have been downright stressful. But still, I can help him. Do you think when they put me back in, it's possible to aim me at Jacksonville, Florida in that same time?"

"Mr. O'Toole, I admire the leaps you have made in your treatment—empathy, connections with other people, pride in work. You have met my highest hopes for you. However, Life Modification Therapy was designed for criminal rehabilitation, not for trying to change the past. The rules and regulations are founded on copious research. Small everyday changes have little effect on future events. Like taking pebbles out of a stream doesn't change the course of the water. But move some boulders, the stream is permanently affected. Life and Death are boulders. I did some research. He was never found."

"But—"

"Even if we had the technology, finding him would be a boulder. We would have no idea what effect this life change would have on the course of current events. That's why it's just not possible. I think it's wonderful you have such concern for him, though. That means you are benefitting from Life Modification Therapy. But one of the reasons we move candidates from country to country on a daily basis is to keep the changes to the time stream as pebble changes. The longer you are in an area, the greater the risk of boulder changes. I know it can all be very confusing. Perhaps you would benefit from more counseling before we reinsert you into the system," she says almost to herself as she scrolls through the holopad.

Goals 2 and 3. Goals 2 and 3. Goals 2 and 3. "No ma'am. I can see what you're sayin'. I guess I did get a little caught up 'cause he reminds me of me. But you're right. I don't know what helpin' him would do to the time creek. Maybe it would dam up, and we'd have no fish."

"I'm glad you understand. You can go back to your cell. I need to write up my recommendation, but I'm very positive about this interview. I'm going to request a sentence reduction. This experience has been very traumatic for you, and I hope the board of governors agrees with me."

"I'd be happier than a galluden with a kwit if that happened!"

"I'll be in touch with you soon, Mr. O'Toole."

"Soon" in prison time equals about a day on Venus, which, for those who didn't pass fifth-grade science, is 243 Earth days. So, more waiting. I'm pretty sure it counts as cruel and unusual punishment.

III

"**Y**ou are one handsome devil, Smullian." I wink at myself in the mirror. Ms. Anemic Heart got me a suit for my board meeting today. Three hundred years of fashion since the twenty-first, and some things don't change. A suit is a suit is a suit. The jackets may get shorter, longer, wider, but they're still jackets. This year designers produced narrow coats, without lapels, that fall below the hips, which compliment my wiry, athletic frame. The pants, equally slim, make me into one tall drink of water. The designers' fabric pattern fails with some weird gray blocks on the shoulders. Geometrics dominate the scene this season. There's not enough color to coax out the green in my hazel eyes.

I wonder what Lydia would think if she saw me out in the world. Is this the kind of guy that turns her head? I may be in a suit, but I still have shaggy hair, an impish gleam in my eye, and a lopsided smile that says, "I'm trouble."

"Who am I kidding? Every girl loves a bad boy cleaned up," I say, shooting myself some Blue Steel in the mirror. Yarsk prison holds a beauty pageant every three years; the winning male and female inmates receive early release. Really, anyone with teeth has a fighting chance. I'd win hands down. But I digress.

"I don't want release. I want back into the system. Ha! What inmate in his right mind has ever said that." I chuckle. "Time to lose Smullian and find Aww Shucks Guy."

With a shudder, I pull my hair into a ponytail. Ms. Anemic Heart thought it would make me look respectable; I'm pretty sure it makes me look neutered. I dismantle the perfect half-Windsor knot I had assembled and tie a sloppy four-in-hand, leaving the narrow end hanging lower than the wide end. I unbutton the jacket and loosen my tightly tucked-in shirt. A great grifter knows how to fit into any echelon of society; a bad one like Aww Shucks Guy has no idea how to dress like a gentleman.

Just as I finish, the guards show up. They slap a neutralizer at the base of my skull (handcuffs are so last century) and lead me to the board of governors. I'm not on trial. After three agonizing weeks and four days, I will finally know if I can see Lydia and David again. Today, they deliver the findings of their audit/investigation of the Life Modification System. While they've been cycling like hamsters in a wheel looking for answers to a scenario that doesn't have a logical conclusion, I've been confined to my cell, thinking—a lot. Mostly about blue Gatorade.

As the guards march me toward the board of governors' assembly, my mind flashes back to that stupid bottle, one-third full. When I came to in that forsaken pit, I clocked that blue liquid almost immediately. I drank from it on and off throughout the day. Valiantly, I rationed it and, for the most part, with success. But there were times when the need won, and I drained more than I planned. It could be the results of those hallucinations and the sickness talking, but I don't think the level of Gatorade changed all day.

Beyond that, how could there be any left in the first place? Davey had been trapped down there three days before I hitched in. Three days of pain, infection, hunger, thirst, and Florida heat. "Sweat Lodge" describes that pit. How did a scared fifteen-year-old kid have the self-control not to drink it all? The only reason I didn't was years of discipline honed by periodic starvation—first at home and then on the streets. I've done without my whole life. I'm used to a rumbly tumbly. Davey's not. That kid has never missed a meal.

The gray man said, "I sustain him." I've heard about Jesus multiplying the loaves and fishes. Pure hogwash, I'd said. But now... *What about the blue Gatorade? Did the Father make that last? I wonder. The religion port better give me some answers.*

We reach the assembly, an imposing room meant to look warm with wood accents on the massive furniture, but the decorators missed the mark. It all looks even more imposing. The guards push me into a seat next to my Life Modification treatment specialist. Behind a raised platform sit the nine members of the board, all human as Life Mod is an earthly justice system. I expected this to be a long, drawn-out brouhaha, but one look at their faces, er, the tops of their heads, tells me I am wrong. No one wants to make eye contact with me or each other. They studiously stare at the desk in front of them. I assume notes reside under their eyes but can't be sure. *They're embarrassed.*

"This won't take long," I mutter.

"What did you say, Mr. O'Toole?" asks Ms. Anemic Heart.

I fiddle with my tie. "I was just wondering how long this was going to be," I whisper.

"It shouldn't take long. Remember, you've done nothing wrong," she reassures me.

"I feel silly in this monkey suit." It never hurts to bring out Aww Shucks Guy.

"You look nice. Don't worry."

I'm not worried. The board members don't know what went wrong. They want this buried, under wraps, finito. They want me out of their sight and back in the system. They want it over. This will be the shortest hearing in the history of government oversight.

What I assume is the chairman of the board, although too old and tubby to be confused with Frank Sinatra, calls my ward number. "SO51399, please stand." I obey, scraping my chair on the floor with a loud screech for effect. The room is just too dang quiet and serious. I straighten my already smooth jacket. "SO51399, after thorough investigation, it is the conclusion of this board that you are without collusion in the malfunction of the Life Modification System. While you did violate Life Modification protocols during said time, said violations were deemed necessary for the protection of the Life Modification System. No penalty will be levied against inmate SO51399 for said transgressions. Furthermore, to mitigate any pain and suffering that might have resulted from said malfunction, inmate SO51399's sentence of 1000 days of Life Modification will be reduced to 970 days, of which 780 days have been served. The remainder of SO51399's sentence is 190 days to be served forthwith. SO51399, you are dismissed."

With that, Ol' Blue Eyes and the rest of the board stand and vamoose out of the room. I'd be willing to bet there are skid marks behind the podium. I was right about them wanting to get as far away from this as possible.

"Good news," says Ms. Anemic Heart. "They reduced your sentence. I was hoping for forty-five days, but I won't sneeze at thirty days."

"What did he mean by 'forthwith'? I'm just real eager to get in there and get it over. You know, get on with that new life me and you talked about."

"I'm so glad to see the change in you, Mr. O'Toole," she pulls out her holopad. "They'll notify me the particulars, but my feeling is they'll want to reinsert you in the next day or two."

Finally, maybe I can get back to Davey and Lydia.

"And there's no idea where I'll be going?"

"No, although we all feel it will be best to place you as far from Florida as we can. You've been through a lot." She places her hand on my shoulder. "We don't want to make things any more difficult for you."

There's a reason I'm the best. I have to sell this with all I have. "I appreciate that. Don't suppose you could put in a good word for Hawaii or one of them rich resorts?" I chuckle.

"Well, I can't do that Mr. O'Toole, but is there anything else I can do for you?"

"Maybe I should, uh, run by that religion port before I get hooked back up."

IV

So, the port is offline for upgrades. That fits right in with the way things have been going. I've been waiting, which is my least favorite thing, all this time to get the skinny on the Father and—nada. No answers for you, pal. Figure it out yourself. *I wonder if that's the way he wants it.*

I think back to when I passed the neuro. Doc delivered the news himself, sitting by my bed again. "Congratulations. I feel much better about your prognosis. I don't think there will be any lasting effects from the emergency reintegration or the system failure that made it necessary."

I knocked on my own head. "I'm a pretty tough egg to scramble."

"I believe that, Mr. O'Toole," he said, getting up to leave. "I've also cleared you to visit the religion port any time you choose."

"Thanks, doc. It's my next stop."

"Good." He smiled, causing those jowls to wiggle. "I'm sure my friend looks forward to hearing from you."

Only the port wasn't my next stop. "Any candidate associated with or involved in an audit of or ongoing investigation into the proper functioning Life Modification Therapy systems and databases will be restricted from all outside communications until such time as the audit or investigation is complete." In other words, no port for me until *They* were satisfied I hadn't somehow jacked the system and engineered myself an all-expense paid trip to Jacksonville, Florida. If *They* had ever been to Jax, *They* wouldn't be investigating me. It's hot, muggy, flat, huge, and boring. Why would anyone want to go there?

I mean the only thing interesting in JaxVegas is, well, the people. I'd engineer all of this *now*. To help David, to see Lydia's blue eyes again. Heck, to hang out with Chuckles one more time. But I wouldn't have done it then. Not for a million dollars. Back then, all I wanted was to serve my time and get back to what I do best. What do I want now? I want to get back to that hot, muggy, flat, huge, boring purgatory. More than anything. And I think there's only one person that can get me there.

"I have no idea how to do this," I pray. "The chip in my head has a whole lot about Christianity. Some of it contradicts. I can't even get to the port to get some straight answers. But here's what I do know. You exist, Father to the Fatherless. You're powerful enough to override a system as complex as Life Mod without leaving a trace. That's impressive. Somehow you are here with me, but you are also with David. He's three hundred years in the past. Plus, you're walking the hospital corridor with younger me right now. Like time means nothing to you. It hurts my head to think about it. The Life Mod people aren't interested in helping Davey—even if they could. He doesn't matter to them, but I know he matters to you. As long as I'm shooting straight here, you're one scary dude. I don't know if you're God or some guy so far in the future what you can do seems godlike. But all the people I've come to care about believe you're the one and only God, so I'm going to roll with that for now. Can you please help David? When they put me back in, can you get me to him, please? I'm saying please here, and, if you know me like you say you do, you know I don't beg. I'm begging though. Help us please."

The lights wink out. Bedtime. I lay back on my bunk, exhausted. What now? I've rolled over and shown my belly to the dominant creature. My heart bangs against my rib cage as the seconds loom into eons while I wait to see if I will be eviscerated or if my trust will be rewarded. In the darkness, I hear, "This is God, whose dwelling is holy."

Bright and early, Pudge Pot drags me out of bed and to the integration floor. *They want me out of here bad.* Before I know it, I'm prepped and ready, hooked up to a bazillion wires and doodads. The docs and nurses patiently explain everything about my body's active hibernation and my mind's electrical transfer, but I don't listen. Last time, I was fascinated, pumped, ready for the great adventure. I couldn't wait to see who I would be, where I would be. This time, I'm nervous. I'm putting my trust in a faceless entity. I know he's real, but I'm still not sure he has my best interests at heart. No one is in the room. There's not a sound monitor, so I go for it.

"You know trust isn't really my strong suit," I pray. "I'm stressin' out. I don't stress out because I rely on me, and I'm the best. But now I have to rely on you, and I don't know you. I could use a little help here." I hear a squeak as the procedure room door opens.

"How are you holding up, Mr. O'Toole?" I can't see as my head is strapped down, but only one man in the whole building calls me by my name—Doc Hounddog.

"A little rattled, Doc."

"That's why I'm here. I want to oversee everything personally. Make sure there are no hiccups this time."

"Pssht. It's not that, Doc. I'm still worried about my friends."

"These the friends that know my Friend?"

"Yep. I talked to him about 'em. I just...I ain't used to trustin' people, especially ones I can't, you know, see or touch."

He gives my hand a squeeze. "He's never failed me."

"Thanks, Doc."

"It'll be a few more minutes, and you'll be back to the twenty-first century." The door shrieks, and he's gone again.

"So how is this supposed to work between us?" I pray. "What am I? Your servant? 'Cause no one tells me what to do. What do you expect from me? The information on the chip all seems to agree on the concept of loving you and loving others. But what does that even mean? Love? I'm not exactly familiar with the concept. I've always viewed it as a weakness."

"SO51399, inhale deeply and hold." A feminine voice emits from an intercom. I inhale and breathe a memory of my mom. I'm about eight, and Dad had once again drunk up all the grocery money. Mom had managed to find some old bread in the back of the pantry. There were only a couple of slices. She scraped the remnants of jelly from the side of the jar and spread them over the stale slices and handed them to me. I wolfed one down greedily before realizing she didn't have any.

"Here, Mommy," I said, handing her the other piece.

"I'm not hungry, Smully," she answered as she ruffled my hair.

"Exhale," the voice continues. I start to get drowsy.

I'm back at the cop shop where I met Lydia. She had been crying, I thought she looked like a plague victim. She told me about selling her parents' house. "In this market, we were very blessed to find a buyer quickly. I put the money aside for David's college." I remember thinking she was nuts. What twenty-one-year-old puts a huge chunk of change in savings—for someone else?

"SO51399, inhale deeply and hold," the voice asks again. This time it sounds a little like Lydia.

A quote from *Phraseology, Jargon, and Mores of Twenty-first Century Earth* scrolls through my head: "Christianity's foundation is that original sin and all subsequent sin separates man from God. In order to reconcile this separation, God sent His son Jesus Christ as a sacrifice to pay the punishment of said sin."

"Exhale," the voice says from far away.

"Sacrifice," I mutter as my mind uncouples from my body. "Love means sacrifice."

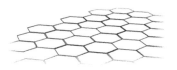

PART SIX

LOVE BREAKING THE RULES

My lids stand at attention. It's dark, but my eyes make out shapes that can only be furniture. *Whew, it's not the pit.* I click on a lamp and stumble out of bed, clinging onto the contents of my host's stomach by sheer willpower, looking for something, anything that can give me my twenty. Unfortunately, my host doesn't have a cell phone, calendar, or even loose piece of mail hanging around his neat as a pin bedroom.

"Curse you for being so orderly," I mutter through clenched teeth. I spy the television remote and head for it when the burning chum rising in my throat refuses to back down any longer. I abandon my mission and dash to the bathroom. I don't quite make it over the john before the bile makes its escape. Most of it lands in the desired location, but the floor will need mopping.

"Later." That has to wait, as well as the usual examination of my pajamas. *Where* and *When* are far more important than *Who* in regard to my current host. I remain in the loo longer than I want to, but also don't want to have to deal with any more gastric goo than necessary. After the churning has subsided, I beat it back to the TV remote. One quick push of the button and local news appears. WTLV, Jacksonville's NBC affiliate. I do a little dance and wait for the date to crawl by at the bottom of the screen. When it does, my legs give way, and I fall to my knees in relief.

"You did it! I'm here. I'm actually here!" He did it. The Father somehow overrode Life Mod and sent me back to Jacksonville the day after I left it. I may have been back in the twenty-fourth a hair over five weeks, but here it's been less than twelve hours. I look to the ceiling, "I've said it before. You're kind of scary. I'm glad you're on my side, 'cause I'd hate for you to be against me. What's the plan? I really hadn't thought past this point because, well no offense, I didn't believe…" *I wasn't sure you were really there. I thought it was too good to be true. Every orphan dreams of a big, mighty Daddy who'll come and adopt them, but we know it will never really happen. But you happened.* "All this mushy stuff is wasting time. We need to rescue David. So, what's the plan?" Several moments pass. No disembodied voices, no strangely apropos memories popping into my head, and no quotes from the chip in my brain make an appearance. Silence oozes across the room.

"Hello? You got anything to add here? 'Cause I could use the help."

Nothing.

"Really? You've been Chatty Cathy for weeks, and at this critical juncture you choose to be silent." I'm up and pacing now.

The news anchors mumble in the background. I look up at the ceiling again and emphatically throw my hands up, but no great insight makes its way to me. "Fine. I get it. You say you'll never leave, that you're right there with me, but you're not, are you? I can handle this myself like I do everything."

I storm off into the bathroom because that's where I always start my day, and it's the only thing I can think of to do. In my huff, I forget about the present I left myself and step dead center in the vomit. It's cold now and slightly viscous, clinging to my foot as I jerk it free.

"Perfect. Nose to the grindstone, Smullian. You can't help David running around half-cocked." I notice for the first time my host's knees are not overly-crazy about bending. "Arthritis?" I grab a towel, handling my foot and then the floor. Then I check out what I'm wearing. Routine is good. Routine brings calm. Routine puts the body on autopilot and allows the mind to work unfettered. White t-shirt and cotton pajama pants. Modest but not Marvin-level propriety. That plus the knees means I must be an older guy. A quick exam of his hands confirms my hunch. They're gnarled, but still have a few more miles to go. Rifling through his medicine cabinet reveals a modest amount of prescription bottles. "Bet he has one of those 'days of the week' pill boxes somewhere. Kitchen." I read one of the labels. "Henry Brown. Strong baby boomer name."

So far, no sweet concerned elderly woman has come knocking to see if I'm—Henry is— okay. I've certainly made enough ruckus to bring someone running even if she'd been asleep in the next room. *Widower?* I doubt he was a lifelong bachelor. Glacier blue eyes stare at me from the mirror. With silver hair atop square-jawed face, I see what Buddy Holly would have looked like if he had the chance to age. "Nope, this handsome guy was definitely not a bachelor."

I step out of the bathroom and to the closet. A quick exam yields athletic suits, sedate Hawaiian shirts—*I didn't think it possible, but these are tasteful, yet still Florida*—starched no less, and long sleeve button-ups with various subtle patterns. *He's got good taste for an old guy. A little more toned-down than Benny and me, but well-put together.* I pick a Hawaiian with a palette of blues and put it on with some ironed jeans. *Very modern Southern gentleman.* While dressing, my mind drifts and the current problem comes tumbling out.

"I'll just—I'll just what? Call the tipline and tell them David is in the building where the fairies fight the mole people? Oh yeah, they'll jump right on that one! That tip will just get shuffled to the bottom of the whackadoo file." I pace the room instinctually studying the pictures on the wall and dresser top. Lots of Henry and the Missus. In all, his outgoing grin shines through. A double frame shows a young Buddy Holly looking kid with his even younger-looking bride. The adjacent frame pictures them much later. *Fiftieth anniversary. Long time. He must miss her to have all these pictures out. No kids. Just him and Mrs. Smiley. I wonder if it was choice or nature.* I rifle through the assortment of things on his bedside table. Hearing aids. *Too much rock n roll, Smiley?* Landline phone with charger base. *He's showing his age.* A Robert Parker novel. *A simple and direct guy. No fluff for him. I wonder if he's ex-military?* A large-print Bible. *I'm just delaying the inevitable.*

"I have to talk to Lydia." Normally, I'd love any excuse to talk to her, and, frankly, my lizard brain wants to see her and her body again, but this? "How am I supposed to bring this up? 'So hey, you don't know me, but I need you to take me to the Fairy Kingdom because the mole people are about to make Davey a casualty of war.' That'll have the same effect as the call to the tipline." I slump backwards onto the bed, puff my cheeks, and blow out the air, Burnsey-style. "Problem 1: Get Lydia to believe me. Can't be a phone call. She'll hang up before I get four words out of my mouth. If I have any chance it needs be face-to-face. Problem 2: I'd have to skip Mr. Smiley's job." I glance back at the ceiling. "Hello? A move like that could get me violated in Life Mod. I just got back thirty days; I don't want to lose them again." The words feel weak coming out of my mouth. I press on. "If I miss work, can you guarantee I won't get caught?" The silence is louder than his voice was the first time he uttered *Father to the Fatherless*. "I barely know the kid. Why should I risk more time for him? Huh?" Again silence. "Besides, what if I do call into his work, what good would it do? What am I supposed to say to Lydia? 'Hello, I'm from the future, and I know where your brother is. Well, you know where your brother is. Come with me to the mole people.' You know what that will get this guy—Baker Acted. A nice 72 hours in a padded cell. You know what it will get this pretty boy? Hard Time! 'Any act which exposes the integrity of Life Modification Therapy will render the candidate's therapy null and void. Said candidate will be returned to his body for alternative punishment.' Telling Lydia the truth is a big no-no. Are you listening to me? Hard Time. You think I should risk everything for a twerp who couldn't tell he was being played? Well, forget it. Uh, uh. No way. He deserved it."

The pregnant silence expands, filling the room. When I was a kid and my mom wanted me to fess up about something, she would stand and stare at me, arms crossed, head tilted, mouth closed. Her eyes would drill into me, exposing the truth. The silence created a vacuum, waiting to be occupied. Before I knew it, the confession would rush out of my mouth, filling the void. I'm eight again, but the truth is far more important than the candy I bought with money I pilfered from her purse. I sit up, hands dangling between my knees.

"He doesn't deserve it. And he's not a twerp. He's a scared kid, who needs help. I can't stand the thought of him down there another second. I'll do it. Are you happy? It seems like you are asking too much. I'm risking everything—my life for all intents and purposes—for someone else I barely know. Violating Life Mod on this scale will get me 'alternative punishment' for who knows how long." I chuckle. "Well, you know. Don't you?" My eyes fall on the large-print Bible. I reach out and flip it open, scanning the table of contents. "But that's the point isn't it? Love is sacrifice."

Whining over, I head downstairs to find out Mr. Smiley's job and call in sick. On the way, I notice a picture of him in uniform with a sizable number of ribbons on his chest. *Army. I was right.* I pat myself on the back. "You are the best, even under extreme stress."

Hanging on the back of a kitchen chair is a bright green apron with a nametag. "Hello, my name is Hank. How can I help you?" it reads. He works at the local grocery.

"By the size of this place, he doesn't need the money," I mutter to myself as I scroll through his phone looking for the number. "Nah. A guy called Hank who smiles that big is a social creature. He works to get out of the house. I bet the customers love him." I press the appropriate number and the other end rings. A pleasant conversant system leads me to the customer service desk. After seven thousand more rings—*I'm on a timetable, people*—someone picks up.

"This is Hank," I pause, realizing that in my rush I didn't get his last name. *Bad tradecraft.*

"Hank! How are you today?" *Yep, Mr. Social. Everyone loves him.*

"Actually, not good. I've got a stomach bug or something. I can't come in today."

"Oh no! You take care of yourself. Drink plenty of fluids," the peppy voice on the phone recommends.

"I will. Thanks." I hang up the phone.

"I've done it. I've officially violated Life Mod. Now time to go expose it to Lydia and possibly get thrown in a deep, dark pit of my own forever. Go big or go home, Smullian my boy."

In the garage, I find a very fine Cherokee. SUVs aren't usually my thing, but I have to give Hank credit where credit is due. This is a splendid vehicle, impeccably kept. Not even a dead bug dare linger on the shiny white paint. The inside sees a vacuum and polish at least once a week. This baby deserves a longer perusal, but I'm on a deadline. Luckily, Hankster outfitted his Jeep with all the best toys, and I punch Lydia's address into the dashboard GPS. *No comment about me knowing her address off the top of my head.* Directions appear, and I'm surprised, although I shouldn't be at this point, to find she lives a mere five minutes away. I glance up. "Well, Silent Bob, you've amazed me again. And that's really hard to do."

When I put the car in gear, the radio pops on. The DJ is talking. "My pastor, Jason, said something really interesting this weekend. He said, 'When you're taking a test, the teacher is silent, but he's still in the room.' How many times have we said, 'I can't hear God! He's abandoned me!' But that's not the case at all. He's right there. Blows my mind." I punch the knob.

"Testing? Is that what's going on here? I'm being tested? Okay, I've heard you do that kind of thing. But I've only been your servant, follower, whatever, for a couple days. Isn't it a little early for a test? Shouldn't I have some more time under my belt? Not that I'm criticizing or anything."

"In 100 feet, turn left," a crisp, charming, British voice commands.

"Okay baby, I'm turning." I grin. "I guess some students are so superior, you put them on the advanced track." One more turn and boom! I'm at her modest apartment complex. I roll past the sad playground and pull into a parking space at her building.

II

"I could still use some support in this conversation," I say. I've spent all my life getting people to believe outrageous lies, but here I am about to pull out all my powers to get her to believe an outrageous truth. 1) Hook her with a known fact. 2) Details add validity. 3) Don't leave room for objection.

I stand outside her door. About a thousand different emotions threaten to burst me open and turn me inside out. Not to mention all, I mean ALL, of the emotions surrounding what I'm about to do. Added to that are my very confusing feelings about Lydia. Women have been commodities to me, and I've been a commodity to them. But this woman...I do a Burnsey inhale, exhale, and knock on the door.

She opens it immediately. She doesn't look any different than she has any other day, but her radiance overwhelms me. For a moment, I can't speak, which is good because she does. "Hank? What are you doing here?"

Of course, she knows Hank. Everyone the Father has sent me to has known Lydia and David in some way. I should have thought of that.

Genius, actually, she will be more apt to take all this weirdness from someone she already knows, likes, and trusts. The Father really does know what he's doing.

"Um, this is going to sound really weird. But I know where David is. Well, you know where David is."

"What do you mean?"

"He's trapped in one of those buildings where you guys pretend the fairies and mole people live."

Her eyes track up and left. She's knows what I'm talking about. Then her brows narrow. "How do you know this?"

I want so badly to just say "God told me," but that's not right. He wants me to lay it on the line.

"This is the weird part. As if that wasn't weird enough. I'm from the future. We brain-hitch. Put our minds in people in the time we want to go to." She is staring at me hard. I rush on. "Monday I was in Marvin Shoemacher, your—"

"My accountant," she mutters.

"Yeah, you saw him at the cop shop, remember. His car was stolen. Anyway, Tuesday I was Benigno, the cop. Wednesday, I was Burnsey, the teacher. We searched all over. Hung up flyers."

Her eyes are fixed on me. "Yeah, we did. Have you been following me? Are you a stalker? Are you involved in what happened to David?" She whirls around and runs to the door. "I'm calling the detectives."

"Wait. Wait." I scramble after her, which is tough with the cane. It's a miracle I don't trip. I slam Hank's gnarled hand on the door, keeping it from closing. "Al's pizza—"

"What?"

"At Al's the other night, we talked about your faith and the Father being a shelter in the storm—"

"You're listening to me, too!"

"No, I couldn't. Think about it. We had the restaurant to ourselves. No one was close enough to overhear."

"You could have used some kind of bug."

"No. Our decision to eat was spontaneous. We were at the restaurant in a few minutes. For Hank to plant a bug, he would have had to have somehow been listening in my car and overhear us choose the restaurant. Then he'd have to rush over there, plant the bug, and get out before we arrived. How could he have done that?" *Classic misdirection. Get her thinking about the impossibility of a bug and not thinking about the possibility of parabolic mics or listening devices on her person.*

"That does seem pretty impossible, but—"

"I know this all sounds nuts, but so does any other explanation. Does it make more sense that the bag boy from the grocery store has an elaborate network of listening devices and spies watching you? That only happens on television. From that standpoint, me being from the future isn't that farfetched. Remember that fake psychic we saw at the park. I knew she was involved somehow, but I didn't know how until Thursday when I was inside David."

She inhales and holds her breath. She wants to believe, but at the same time, she wants to call the men with the straight jacket.

"Bronwen, the psychic, told Davey she would do a seance to call your Mom and Dad. He took the money to pay for it. She lured him there to steal from him. When he caught on, she pushed him—hard. He fell from the third to the first floor, breaking his leg and ribs. I only know where the place is because he wrote you a letter and he talked about the fairies and moles. He wrote, 'It's funny to me how many times we drove by these buildings and made up stories about the fairy creatures that lived here and their wars with the mole people. I hoped something magical would happen here and, instead, I got ripped off and trapped in this empty, sad place.'"

"Look, this is all—"

"I know it sounds like I've slipped into full-on dementia, but what have you got to lose? Call Detectives Diaz and Weidhoff. Have them meet us there. We'll go in separate cars. And I'm old. You can take me if I try anything. Don't you want to save David?" *Grifter trick 856, ask a question someone would never say no to.*

"Okay. I'm not giving you directions or an address. You'll have to follow. And I AM calling them." Feisty girl takes charge. I love it.

"Cool. I'm in the white SUV."

Pretty soon we're speeding down San Jose. She's driving like it's the grand prix in that dilapidated VW. I respect a woman who knows how to handle her wheels. We pull into a once- cleared, but now overgrown lot with some run down, half-finished condominiums off San Jose. *He's been ten minutes down the road this whole time. So close, yet it could have been a galaxy away for the chances of anyone finding this place.* It feels right, but I won't know which building until I see inside.

"I prayed about this the whole way over. Every bit of it seems crazy. But I'm not scared. The Spirit is giving me peace. So, I'm giving you this a chance. You better be right." Lydia's eyes imply some sort of violence will occur if I don't deliver.

You got this, Father? I silently pray. I'm banking all I have on you.

I scan the property. Which building would make the most sense for a grifter? One in the back, of course. More privacy. But Bonehead Bronwen's laziness and lack of skill would lead her elsewhere. Would she be stupid enough to use the first building? Maybe. Probably. I point. "Let's try this one." We run toward it.

Lydia educates me between breaths, "The developer ran out of funds. They've been sitting here like this for years. David and I imagined these transported you to another realm like Narnia or guarded a secret world like Fablehaven. That's how the stories grew. Only he and I know about that."

Desperate to justify her trust, I dash up the building's steps as fast as old man Hank's arthritic knees will take me. Lydia hangs back. Her faith in me and my insane story are hanging by a thread. I enter the second apartment and, miracle of all miracles, find what I was looking for. (When do things ever work out on the first try?) A giant hole occupies the middle of the floor with a faint drawing of a pentagram next to it. I lean out the door. "This is the one." Her speed picks up. I dash back to the hole and shine a flashlight Hank had in his glove box in the darkness. "David!"

No response. When I redirect the light, I can see the edge of his boot.

"David!"

Now, Lydia is beside me on her knees. Light streams into the hole.

"David!" Our voices in chorus.

We hear a weak whisper, an incoherent mutter.

"David, it's me," Lydia shouts. "Please, please answer," she whispers.

"His ribs are damaged, remember? Yelling might be hard." I say to her. "David bang one of the bottles on the floor if you can hear us," I scream into the hole.

The boot moves slightly, and we hear the empty thud of plastic on the concrete. It comes again louder.

"We're getting help," Lydia yells.

The banging continues. Together we stumble down the stairs to the first floor. The door is boarded closed, as expected. Lydia pulls fruitlessly at the wood, cutting her hands.

"David," she yells through the door. "I'm here. I'm right here. Help is on the way. They'll be here any minute. Just hold on."

We hear the plonking of the bottle from inside. His fervent yes and SOS. She calls the boys in blue again. "We found him. He's trapped. He's hurt bad." She hangs up. "They're calling a bus. I guess that's an ambulance." She looks at me, tears in her eyes. "You were right. If you're right about this…"

"I'm right about all of it. Crazy and insane I know, but everything I've told you is true."

"But how?"

I shrug. "I don't understand all the techy stuff."

"So, they sent you from the future to find David?"

"No, they sent me from the future to be 'exposed to law-abiding and virtuous citizens.' Someone, I think your God, sent me to find David."

"I don't understand."

"Me either. I never believed in god, but, well, it's been a weird week. I think he did it, all this for you and David…and maybe me. Remember talking to Mr. Burns the other night about his friend the orphan?"

"Yes. I'm trying to wrap my mind around this. So that was you, some time traveler, and not him?"

"I'm not a time traveler. I'm a felon. It's a rehab program for prisoners. But, yeah, it was me. Anyway, I was telling you my story. I lost my mom at twelve. Been on my own ever since. Anyway, I'm thinking that your god chose me for this job specifically, to help me in some way. I'm not sure why he'd bother. I'm not exactly a stellar candidate."

"He cares about everyone. He created us all. We're all his children."

I snort. "I'm not sure how I feel about all that. It's new to me. It's not like I've had the best life. It seems like a strange way to treat children. You've lost your parents, brother, and now this. Didn't seem like love at first, but at the same time here I am, leading you to David. He's confusing, that Father to the Fatherless. I don't understand it all."

"His ways are not our ways. His logic and our logic don't mesh. Instead of giving us righteous punishment for our sin; he sent his son as a sacrifice so we that could have a relationship. It doesn't make sense. I suppose this makes as much sense as other things he's done. Shadrach, Meshach, and Abednego survived a fiery furnace without a scratch. Job. Elijah went up in a whirlwind." She's quiet for a moment. I know she needs a minute, so I give it to her. A grifter knows when to talk, and when to keep his yap shut.

"It's funny," she continues. "I haven't had a check in my spirit about any of this. My mind has plenty of questions, but, in my spirit, it feels true. Faith is all about trusting in what you can't see or touch. And I feel like God is saying I can trust you, as illogical as that may be."

The screech of brakes resonates from the parking lot. A whining siren blares in the distance, looming closer. Lydia says, "Help is here, little brother! Hold on a few moments more."

"You should go meet them. They don't know me from Adam's Housecat. I'll stay with Davey."

She darts out to the parking lot. I hear her talking with Benny Boy and Chuckles.

"Sorry, I took so long," I say through the door; then creep into the dark of a stairwell. They don't need to see me. There would be too many questions to answer. I mean to fade out entirely, but I want to see David with my own eyes. Make sure he'll be okay.

Lydia must have explained because Chuckles appears with a tire iron. He slips one end under a board and pulls with all his might. The warped wood groans under the pressure but doesn't give. Benny grabs the handle lower down and together they wrestle the board off. All the boards are cleared in a matter of moments, the door won't open.

"Something is blocking it," Benny says.

"David, if you're leaning on the door, try to move over, okay?" Lydia says.

We hear a sharp moan of pain and some scuffling inside. Benny tries the door again, and it swings open. David, who no longer has the strength to hold himself up, collapses into the entryway. He looks like he's already dead. Slack skin clings to his cheekbones and jaw. His eyes are sunken. Benny checks for vitals. Lydia is crying and holding his hand. Charlie dashes into the parking lot with his football speed to meet the approaching ambulance. The paramedics arrive and do their thing. The seconds go on for eternity. Finally, they load him on the gurney.

"He's so pale. Why are his lips blue?" I hear Lydia whisper.

"We're taking him to the trauma center at Shands," one of the paramedics says to Benny. I slink out of the back of the development. Once they are clear, I head back to Hankster's car. The day is almost half over, and I still have a lot of work to do.

III

Good thing my quarry lacks an abundance of brains. She should have blown town the day things went south with Davey. A good grifter would. Not only did she stick around, but I had found her at the scene of the crime! She went back to the same park where she picked up Davey two days after she dumped him. It's clear by her specialty in the conning trade and that amateur move, that she's devoid of imagination. She'll stick to what she knows. However, once a bunch of jackboots start tromping through her territory with a frighteningly accurate drawing of her, she'll bolt.

I need to find her before they spook her. Besides, she's mine. I want the satisfaction of bringing her in, not them. I decide she would have had enough survival instincts to avoid Mandarin Park after our—hers and Burnsey's—conversation. So, I'm not going to waste time searching there. But I bet she'll stick to the southside of Jacksonville, near, but not in Mandarin.

Hank is dressed to impress, and I've got a mission. First few parks are duds, but then I find her. Perched upon a picnic table doing the meditation thing, like a sitting duck. I walk past her slowly with my cell phone to my ear, feigning a call.

"Gabby can you pull up the Riverwalk Condo papers? I drove by that development disaster on San Jose this morning, and there were cop cars and an ambulance outside one of the them. I'm going to have to come into the firm today and double check the docs as far as liability for the empty buildings. And have Howard call the police station and see what he can find out. So much for a day off." *Now if she had time to really think she might wonder why I was in the park making a call instead of running into the office…but she won't really think. She'll be in panic mode. That's a conman's bread and butter—make your prey feel desperate, so they don't have time to really think.* "There's only limited spots, you could lose out on this once in a lifetime opportunity if you don't act now!"

I end the call and sit at the table next to hers. Pretending to scroll through my contacts, I watch her in my peripheral vision. She's cocked her head in my direction.

"Excuse me kind sir, I would never eavesdrop, but did you say there were official vehicles at those dilapidated buildings on San Jose?"

"Yep, this is a total train wreck. I don't need this six months before retirement."

"The ones near the creek?"

"Yeah, lady. Can I get on with my calls?"

"Certainly, if you wouldn't mind entertaining one more question."

"Sure, I'm loaded with time." *Being irritated increases her stress and, also, draws her in because she has to work for it. Nobody trusts something easy.* "Sorry sir, the last slot just filled. Maybe next time."

"No, please, can't you squeeze me in?"

"Sure, maybe we can wiggle some room in Platinum status, but that's an extra $200."

"Deal!"

"Are you involved in the financing of those residences?"

"No, I lucked out there. They took a bath. I'm the lawyer."

Her eyes brighten with hope.

"Can I disturb you with one more, hypothetical question?"

"Oh yeah, I love giving legal advice on my day off when a giant bomb is about to explode in my face."

She giggles lightly and picks at the fringe on her gypsy skirt. "What if someone accidentally without malice hurt someone and didn't get help?"

"Was it during the commission of a crime?"

"Excuse me?"

"Was it during the commission of a crime?" I punctuate each word like she's hard of hearing, applying more stress.

"What if the crime were very small one?"

"Lady, it doesn't matter if you stole a stick of gum. Battery during the course of a crime adds time. Plus, you said, 'hurt.' How badly? That could be Aggravated Battery, which is a whole other ball game. But you're a skinny, little thing. A good lawyer could convince a jury you damaged the dude in self-defense." Now, she's biting her perfect nails. *Tick, tick, tick. The pressure increases.*

"What if the person were a teenager?"

"How old?"

"14 or 15."

"Jury would still consider that a kid, and they come down hard on anyone that hurts a kid. Especially a good-looking one. Sounds cold, but it's true." Her eyes dart around the park as if she's expecting the boys in blue to materialize out of thin air. She rubs frantically at her skirt and starts to rise. *Here's where I have to be careful. Don't want her to explode. Time to be her friend. Punishment and reward, punishment and reward. It's a time-honored grifting technique.*

"You in trouble?" I ask.

"Huh."

"Let me give you some free advice. Running is never a good idea. You don't want to add 'Fugitive from Justice' to your mounting charges, plus you spend the rest of your youth looking over your shoulder. If you need help, solicit a lawyer."

"Okay, here's the thing—" *Time to turn the heat back up.*

"Ah, ah. Hold up, sweetie. I'm not your lawyer unless you've given me a retainer."

"A retainer?"

"A fee paid to retain professional advice. Without a retainer, I'm a witness. With a retainer, you have attorney-client privilege."

"How much?"

"My usual is $2000."

"I don't have that much." Her eyes plead with me.

"Then check the yellow pages. I'm sure you'll find someone within your budget. Of course, they probably got their degree online." I stand up and walk away. I can hear her sandals slapping the pavement as she pursues me.

"Wait, wait. I've got five hundred. I could give it to you now."

I sniff and purse my lips. "All right. I could write you off as a charity case." *Punishment, reward, punishment, reward.*

She digs in the satchel draped across her chest and hands me a wad of bills. I thumb through it, counting each one. I want her to suffer a little as she waits. It's only fair after all David has waited and suffered. I count a second time. She stops breathing. A third time.

"I can't today. I have to deal with this cock-up. Come to my office 11:15 AM tomorrow. Don't be late. I abhor tardiness."

"I won't be."

"Go home and don't leave for any reason. Call me immediately if something happens." I pull out a notebook and jot down a fake firm name, address, and phone. Then I hand it to her. "Write down your legal name, address, and phone number. I need it to start your file."

"Okay," she says complying. *Blanche Evans! No wonder she changed her name.*

"11:15 sharp. And don't talk to anyone," I say as I walk away. Later, she'll call that number, and no one will answer. The help she's waiting for won't come, and she will rot in jail. *It's better than she deserves.*

I hightail it to the Jeep. I need to get out of here quick. *When the deal is done, cut and run.* If that cow sees me in the parking lot, it will ruin the illusion. I drive away and think about my next move. I can't call the tip line from Hank's cell; they might trace it and question him later. I don't want to bring that mess down on him. I scan both sides of the road for a viable place to make the call. Unfortunately in this century, pay phones have gone the way of the dodo. So, I need to find a business, but one that would have some privacy near the phone. This convo can't be overheard. I spy a small salon.

"That'll do. Small salons don't generally have a receptionist. If it doesn't look right when I walk in, I'll find another place."

It's perfect. There are only two stylists in the joint. Both working with customers near the back. One looks up at me when I enter. "How can I help you?"

I shake my cell in the air. "I'm out of power and need to check in with the missus. Can I use your phone?"

"Sure," she says, pointing to the reception desk.

"Thank you." I wait until both are distracted with their clients to pick up and dial. After the usual rigmarole, I get to the tip line. Approximating my best hick accent, I say, "My second cousin's ex-girlfriend goes by the name Bronwen Evangelista, which is silly 'cause her Mama named her Blanche. Anyway, she does this whole psychic scheme. I usually don't care how she hustles, but she was bragging about stealing from a kid, and it sounded like she hurt him. You should look into her."

"Do you have a full name and address?"

"I surely do," I read out the info from the notepad.

"What is your name, sir?"

"Oh, I'd rather not say. I ain't no rat, but I draw the line at hurting kids."

"Can you—?"

I hang up before she can ask any more questions.

I wave to the stylists, who wave back, and exit the store. Once in the car, I slide into the plush leather seat, smiling. "I've saved a life and caught a bad guy. Balanced against my petty crimes, I guess that makes us even," I say to the Father. It doesn't feel right though. "I'm not sure Sharila will think these deeds make up for leaving her broke and broken. Or all the other people I fleeced. I doubt they'd say, 'He saved a boy's life. That's so heroic! I don't care about the twenty thou he stole from me anymore.' So then how does it work?

I've got more than a dozen years' worth of nefarious deeds. How would I ever make that right with you?"

"Christianity's foundation is that original sin and all subsequent sin separates man from God. In order to reconcile this separation, God sent his son Jesus Christ as a sacrifice to pay the punishment of said sin." The chip's quote floats through my mind.

"No, things don't work that way. Nothing is ever free. There are strings attached," I think over my time in Jax, from Marvin forward everything that happened to me was orchestrated by the Father. "I guess in reality, the whole week here has been one big string. We get forgiveness, you get a follower."

"Father to the Fatherless," echoes through the SUV.

"Not a follower, a son." I think about my own drunken, abusive, carousing father. "I don't know what it means to be a son. You've spoken to me more than my dad ever did. What do you expect from me?"

"If you love me, obey my commandments."

"I'm not so big on obeying. What if I fail? And what are these commandments anyway? Stupid question. There's a whole book, right? And you definitely have a way of making yourself known." I chuckle. "Wait a minute. I didn't believe you existed at the beginning. How did you know I'd cooperate? Another stupid question. You reached out to me in two different centuries. Time means nothing to you. I imagine you knew what I would do a long, long time ago. That could mess up my brain if I think about it too much."

Suddenly, Hank's stomach announces its presence. With the insistence of Simon's cat, it shouts, "Feed Me!" Now that all the urgency and adrenaline of the day is worn off, I am hungry.

Starving. I skipped breakfast, and it's deep into the afternoon. Nearby, a sign beckons me to bliss—Longhorn. I promised myself a steak days ago, and I'm sure this would be part of Hank's "logical and conventional daily activities." Although that concept has flown the coop, I still want to be mindful of what Hank would do. That's just good tradecraft. Time for the early bird special.

Rare, seared on both sides, tender and juicy in the middle, the sirloin practically melts in my mouth. I gulp down the loaded baked potato in a few mouthfuls, creamy, salty, and sour blending in every portion. Topping it all off, is the dry sweetness of cheesecake. *I hope Hankster isn't a diabetic. I forgot to check his meds.*

As I sip on the last vestiges of my Coke, I ponder my next move. I need to get the cash to Lydia. A smart grifter would drop it in the mail. *When the job is done, cut and run.* And I'm a smart grifter, but this whole situation changed the rules. My every action today has been not only not savvy, but downright dumb. I want to know Davey will be okay. I want to talk to her one more time. I sip again hearing the satisfying slurp meaning I've hit the bottom of the glass. "Dumb, it is."

The cash might be a problem. Knowing Lydia, she won't accept more than was taken, if she accepts the money at all. What to do with the remainder? I spy a church across the street. Wandering over, I find a mail slot in the side door. I take out the notepad and jot, "For the fatherless Psalm 68:5." Wrapping the paper around the remaining $112, I drop it through the slot.

"I kinda wish good deeds counted, 'cause I am on a roll today!" I punch Shands hospital into the GPS and head toward Stupidville.

When I enter the ICU waiting room, Lydia looks up at me with a smile. "It's you."

"How is he?" I ask taking the seat across from her.

"The doctors can't believe he's still alive. They're calling him a miracle. For once, they don't know how right they are. God is good. I'm still in awe. I don't imagine that will change anytime soon."

"What's the prognosis?"

"They've got him on IV antibiotics. They'll need to operate on the ankle when he's stable, but they think they can save it. Fill him with all kinds of hardware. He'll need a lot of PT."

"Ouch. I'm sorry I didn't find him sooner."

"Are you crazy? He's alive because of you. We owe you everything."

"Speaking of owing," I say, handing her the cash.

"What's this?"

"The Rock the Universe money."

"I can't take this from you."

"You're not. Let's just say Blanche, Bronwen, saw the error of her ways and returned it."

"Detective Diaz called me and said they had her in custody. There was an anonymous call on the tipline. That was you?"

"It takes a grifter to catch a con artist."

"Wow! How did you—"

"It wasn't hard. She's not that bright, really. She's a blight on the profession."

"So that's what you're doing time for? Conning people."

"Yes. My mom taught me. It was how we got by."

"You've had such a hard life," she puts her hand on mine. It's soft and warm. *Here she is, in the depths of despair, and she's comforting me.*

"I survived. What's the plan for you now?"

"I have no idea and don't want to think about it anymore. I hear nothing for days, and then the last few hours there's been a glut of information and adrenaline. I'm exhausted. I'd rather talk about you. I have so many questions! What's it like in the future? Is there space travel? Do people fly? Huh, I just realized. You've done so much for us, and I don't even know your name."

I look into her open face and find I'm not afraid. Not even the slightest hint of trepidation stirs. My defenses aren't just down; they're gone. *Is this what it feels like to trust someone?*

"My name is Smullian, an unfortunate moniker given to me by my mother. Its origins have something to do with a pirate and a stolen barrel of Zevekan gin…"

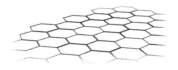

SAME DAY, DIFFERENT THING

An alarm rings from across the room. I stumble out of bed searching for it, change my mind and head to the bathroom. It continues beeping while I take care of my beastly business. *This place isn't much bigger than an airplane bathroom. I'm wedged in here like a semarine in its hole.* I briefly take into account the room, small, orderly, while I track down the source of sound. I find the phone, alarm blaring, on a desk on the far side of the room. *The word 'far' is a bit generous. The desk is barely two feet from the bed.*

A lanyard lies next to the phone. A brown face with dark eyes and a serious smile emits from the surface. "Anand Bhatnagar D.

V., IDC," I read out loud. "IDC? Probably a call center. Ugh. Hope it's not outbound." I shuffle through Anand's very clean desk. *With a place this small, one can't afford to be messy.* Thankfully, I find his password book and work schedule in a matter of seconds. Time is essential. I have somewhere to be before his shift starts. A quick Google search shows me I'm in Bangalore and where I want to go is on the way to IDC.

The chip in my brain tells me that Bangalore's population exceeds New York City's by a few million. "Traffic's gonna be awful. I better high-tail it. I want as much time as I can eek out." Throwing on the nearest set of clothes from the wardrobe, I grab the necessary accoutrements for the day and head out the door. Anand's bright red Hero starts up easily, and soon I'm zipping in and out of the congested traffic on the sleek motorbike.

It's been 41 days since Hank, and The Powers-That-Be at Life Mod don't have a clue about what I did, as far as I know. Not a peep from the future. My program is progressing as normal. 148 days to go. No hiccoughs from the Father, either. Although I am spending a lot of free time reading his word. Research. I put my trust in this guy, or this being, whatever. I need to know all I can about him. I don't always understand it, but more of it makes sense than I thought would. The Bible says that's the Holy Spirit's job. I'm still wrapping my head around the whole Trinity thing.

Horns are not optional here in Bangalore. They are an essential piece of the car's safety equipment. Honking, in dissonant keys, reverberates around me. The sound spurs me on to my destination.

The doctors did save Davey's foot, and he is putting in some grueling hours of PT. But his attitude is baffling to those around him. His brooding manner evaporated after the pit. He doesn't complain or whine and embraces each challenge with a smile. He knows how close he came to death. Madds remains by his side, and the two canoodle to the point of being revolting.

Was that street filled with piles of garbage? Huh. I guess Bangalore has grown too fast for the infrastructure to keep up. Need a landfill? No problem—here's an abandoned street. Nonplussed by his strange actions, Hank felt that the Father had used him that day to accomplish his will. To him, the vague memories only mean that the Holy Spirit was in control. He believes his duties don't end with finding Davey. In essence, he's become Lydia's and David's adoptive grandfather, the three of them creating their own family. Hank often drives Davey to PT and doctor appointments, as well as sharing dinner with the kids multiple nights a week. In fact, there are talks of the Hawthornes moving in with him. That way, Lydia could quit working and go to school full time. Her independent streak makes her a little resistant to the prospect. She doesn't want to take advantage of Hank. I think, in the end, she'll accept the offer.

I reach the internet cafe and trot inside. *Twenty minutes will have to do.* The woman at the counter takes my ID and cash. I sign up for a computer and head to the farthest one from the door. I log into Gmail and enter an address known only by one other person in the world. The inbox indicates mail from *feistygrrl21*. I made the account; I got to pick the username.

I open it.

"Hello Smullian, Who are you today?" It reads.

Who am I indeed?

ABOUT THE AUTHOR

 Nancy Jo Wilson was published in her local paper and won various writing contests in high school, including a scholarship from the state of TN. Her first novel, *Escape the Amoz,* placed second in the science fiction category of the 2009 Do It Write! competition. She blogs about faith and homeschooling on her website, six5mom.com. Nancy's articles have appeared in *Practical Homeschooling* and *MauMag* magazine. Contact her through her website www.nancyjowilsonauthor.com. A Jacksonville, FL native, she now resides in Thomaston, GA with her family.

A free ebook edition is available with the purchase of this book.

To claim your free ebook edition:

1. Visit MorganJamesBOGO.com
2. Sign your name CLEARLY in the space
3. Complete the form and submit a photo of the entire copyright page
4. You or your friend can download the ebook to your preferred device

Print & Digital Together Forever.

Snap a photo

Free ebook

Read anywhere